PRAISE FOR BRENDAN VIDITO

"Surreal, grotesque, erotic. Brendan Vidito is a unique and disturbing new voice."

"Vidito's words squirt shocking psychosexual bug juice into your brain's most private parts."

"Brendan Vidito is the bastard son of Clive Barker and his fresh take on body horror will fuck you up."

T0145506

NIGHTMARES IN ECSTASY

BRENDAN VIDITO

Copyright © 2018 by Brendan Vidito

Cover by Matthew Revert

ISBN: 978-1-944866-23-5

CLASH Books

PO BOX 487 Claremont, NH 03743

PREVIOUSLY PUBLISHED

"Fuck Shock" *Splatterpunk #6* (2015)
"Rebound" *Dark Moon Digest #23* (2016)
"The Androgyne" *Splatterpunk's Not Dead* (2016)
"Placenta Bride" *Forest of Sex and Death* (2017)
"The Black Waters of Babylon" *Dead Bait 4* (2017)
"Piss Slave" *Strange Behaviors: An Anthology of Absolute Luridity* (2018)
"Stag Loop" *Tragedy Queens: Stories Inspired by Lana Del Rey and Sylvia Plath* (2018)
"Earworm" *Zombie Punks Fuck Off* (2018)

CONTENTS

THE ANDROGYNE

Haden and Daphne entered the motel room and dropped their luggage on the floor.

The place was pregnant with a septic-smelling darkness. Curtains were drawn over the window, and the carpet resembled a fungus the color of bad meat. There were two double beds and a long dresser decorated with thick, yellowed candles. Haden recognized it for what it was: a sacrificial altar.

Daphne inhaled a trembling breath. She moved toward the nearest bed. Haden commanded his legs into motion. They sat down as one.

Their flesh, fused at the hip.

Haden's pale flank blended with Daphne's olive-hued skin, meeting in the middle to form a tone unique to their pairing. Their clothes had been specially tailored to accommodate their conjoined body.

They had not always been this way. The unification began shortly after their one-year anniversary. By that time, Haden and Daphne were together almost every waking hour.

Driving home from the movies on a Saturday night, the couple was overtaken by a lustful desire for the other's flesh. They found a secluded roundabout fringed by a forest so thickly leaved it seemed a wall of pure darkness. They clambered to the back seat, dirtying the upholstery with their shoes, and sprawled in a tangle of limbs. Daphne hiked up her skirt and tore a hole in the crotch of her pantyhose. Haden dropped his pants so they hung around his knees. He pulled the crotch of her underwear aside and entered her. The smell of her cunt was like an opiate, clearing Haden's head and filling him with an animal hunger.

They fucked passionately as moonlight trickled through the window, painting their bodies with delicate strokes of white and silver. It made the sweat and cum glittering on their skin look like droplets of a deadly, mercurial poison. As they thrust and grappled, they appeared to become a single organism writhing in death spasm.

When it was over, and they lay together bathed in a hot stew of sex, Daphne let out a shriek of pain and surprise. She looked down between them, where their hips rested side by side. A pale cartilaginous hook had emerged from Haden's skin and was now attempting to pierce her own. The muscles on Haden's hip quivered and swelled, pushing the hook deeper into Daphne. She struggled briefly, taken by a whim of panic, and then Haden placed his hand on her cheek. She calmed down almost instantly. "It's okay, babe," he said. "This is what we want."

She nodded, smiled. The hook sank deeper with a wet fleshy sound. "I love you," she said. He said it back. Their lips pressed together as the hook settled into place with a spastic twitch that reminded them both of an insect. Over the next few months, their flesh adhered around the hook, melding together as one.

Back in the motel room, Haden said, "The sooner we do this, the easier it'll be on the both of us."

He went to stand up, but Daphne wasn't moving. He looked at her and his mind abruptly ceased to recognize reality as a moving sequence of events. Instead, Daphne's movements slowed down, constituting a series of still-lives. Loose strands of her auburn hair were plastered to a freckled brow. Her lips were parted slightly, showing the white of her teeth—arranged to near-perfection by a two-year stint in braces. Her eyes looked toward the altar, the delicate wisp of her lashes framing eyes that were iridescent and flecked with various shades of blue like a living ocean. Once Haden took in every conceivable detail, the still life shuttered and reeled back into motion. Why did it have to come to this? he thought. Why couldn't we just love each other?

"Are you ready, Daphne?"

She wouldn't look at him. "The stuff is in the red duffle."

They stood up together and walked toward the door where they left their bags. After two years of being attached, their shared movement was natural, effortless. They bent down. Haden lifted the red duffle off the floor, and they returned to sit on the bed. Artifacts from their relationship were piled haphazardly inside: the teddy bears they made to resemble one another, photo albums, concert and movie tickets, love letters, handcuffs, jewelry, and sex toys.

They approached the altar and placed each item reverently on the unfinished wooden surface. When the duffle was empty, Daphne hesitated and wrung her fingers together as if trying to mend an invisible object. Then she heaved a lung-emptying sigh and pulled the promise ring off her right ring finger.

Haden watched silently as she placed it among the other artifacts. It met the wood with a dull, inconsequential tap.

Haden opened the duffle's side pocket, pulled out a matchbook and box cutter.

"What is that for?" Daphne said, pointing at the box cutter. Her surprise was audible.

"The Curator said we might need it."

He struck a match and lit each of the five candles.

"Anything else the Curator said that you want to share?" Daphne said with venom.

He had spoken to each of them individually before giving them the key to their room.

"That's all. What did he say to you?"

Daphne hesitated. "That this place is haunted, but not in the way we were conditioned to understand."

Haden shook his head, bewildered. "Whatever the fuck that means."

They sat back down on the bed, simultaneously aware of the

next step in the ritual. They had to repeat the act of union that connected their bodies in the first place.

Haden moved his hand to the small of Daphne's back. He used the other to reach over her as he leaned in for a kiss. She was reluctant at first, her lips stiff and unresponsive, but the longer Haden persisted in his affections, the more willing she became. Her lips opened to him, the pink of her tongue darting wet and slick into his mouth. Haden wrapped her in his arms and together they sank down into the mattress.

His lips moved to her chin, brushing the dip beneath her jaw, to her neck where he gently sucked the prickling skin.

He felt the rumble of her vocal cords against his mouth. Daphne said. "How much longer do we have to do this?"

Haden looked her in the eye, saw the pain there, and said, "I don't know."

He knew his answer wasn't satisfactory. The implication of Daphne's words struck him like a blow. By all rights, this *was* torture. They had come to this hole in the wall to break-up, to sever themselves from one another. This ritual seemed like some-body's idea of a sick joke. Laying out their shit like a sideshow, summoning their final dregs of passion in a cruel act of ceremony.

Haden's grip was tight around Daphne's throat as he pressed his mouth against hers, smothering her, his tongue thrusting deeply. Her lips trembled against his. A tear escaped the corner of her eye and glided down her cheekbone.

That kiss held all the pain and finality of a kiss goodbye.

Haden pulled the sundress over Daphne's head, squeezed her breasts and closed his mouth around each nipple until they were engorged and erect. Daphne grappled frantically with the hem of Haden's t-shirt until he got impatient, wrenched it off and tossed it on the floor. When they lay naked, their bodies sheened in the day's sweat, Haden felt Daphne's warmth envelop him. He sighed like a man lowering into a warm bath.

They tasted each other, the salt of sweat on skin, the faint tang of semen and the warm bitterness of vaginal lubrication. Their fluid mingled in a singular concoction and they drank deeply, a final act of communion. The last feast arranged on a table of clammy flesh, goblets rimmed with enamel or labial tissue and bread sampled with probing tongues.

When it was over, Daphne rolled on her side, with her back to Haden, and started to weep. The bridge of flesh that connected them was flexible enough to allow a modicum of free movement.

"Are we sure this is what we want?"

Haden pressed his body against her back, clutching her stomach from behind.

"It's what we need. We're not happy. Haven't been for a while."

"I hate this."

"Here," Haden said, offering his hand. "Let's wash the day off."

They edged to the side of the bed, sat there for a moment. Daphne wiped away the tears that traced runnels of mascara down her cheeks before standing up.

Inside the bathroom, the septic smell was almost overpowering.

"I think it's coming from under the sink," Haden said. He bent down, feeling a tug as Daphne refused to follow, pulled her down by the arm, and swung the cabinet doors open. The stench nearly knocked them over.

Squatting under the rusted belly of the sink was an animal with oily black skin. It looked like road kill with the shape of a bullfrog, which tapered whitely into something resembling a larva. The face that grinned up at Daphne and Haden was filled with teeth like heroin needles bent out of shape.

"What the fuck is that?" Haden said.

"The catalyst."

"What?" Haden burst out. "Did the Curator say something else to you?"

The animal made a noise halfway between a squeak and a croak and vomited a stream of yellow bile on the couple. As soon as it touched their skin it started to hiss and bubble.

Haden shrieked, clawed at the bile sizzling beside his left eye. Daphne made a low keening sound and wiped away the clumps on her breasts and throat. The force of their struggles sent the couple sprawling to the floor.

The animal retched, ejecting another surge of vomit, splashing the place where their bodies connected.

This was it. The separation had begun.

"Oh fuck, what do we do?" Daphne said. The words came out in a single, panting breath.

"Let it burn through."

The pain was excruciating. The slightest draft felt like a whip against the corroding flesh. The acid bore through muscle and vein, reddening the yellow froth around the wound. It trickled sluggishly and dripped on the floor with a faint plopping hiss.

The acid had melted through half the bridge of flesh, when it reached the hook joining Haden to Daphne. As soon as the first drop touched the hook, something woke up inside Haden, and his body went into revolt.

He screamed as a second hook burst through his shoulder and lunged at Daphne on a feeler of tendinous flesh.

She jerked away. The hook carved a deep gash along the ridge of her clavicle, retreated, and lunged again.

Haden grasped it in mid lash, started to pull. He could feel it tugging uncomfortably in his chest. Then there was a pop, followed by a gush of blood and lymph. The tendon came sliding out like a dead snake. Haden whipped it across the room.

The hook embedded in Daphne's hip started to wriggle as the acid ate it away, sending a wisp of smoke into the air.

A third hook burst out of Haden's thigh, leaving a wide gash. He saw the fourth slither under the skin of his abdomen before it shot out in a vivid spray of blood. The hook wriggled free, spraying the floor and walls with red, and attacked Daphne. It raked her pubis, opening a gushing slit all the way up to her navel before penetrating the skin.

Haden went to pull it out of her, and then remembered the box cutter.

"Quick, this way!" he screamed, as the hook from his thigh lunged at Daphne, struggling for purchase.

Together they crawled naked across the floor, clawing their way into the main area. Once they reached the altar, the hook from Haden's thigh pierced the fatty tissue under Daphne's ass. She yelped in pain.

Covered in blood, looking like an overgrown miscarriage, Haden reached up and snatched the box cutter off the altar. He extended the blade and started cutting the tentacles.

When he was finished, he moved to the leftover flesh connecting his body to Daphne's.

"No!" she screamed, but he ignored her and started cutting anyway.

Daphne bit her lip against the pain. Tears poured down her face. Without even knowing it, she grasped Haden's free hand and squeezed until the skin went white. With a final back and forth sawing motion, they came apart.

Haden moaned loudly and let his upper body slump to the floor. He started to cry, loud choking sobs that threatened to rip his lungs and larynx.

Daphne lay shivering on her back. Her body conveyed a network of tiny red rivers. She had never felt so cold, or so alone.

Slowly, her hand slid out of his.

The Curator entered his private museum, a vast chamber piled high with the artifacts of a million broken relationships. Peering through the eyeholes of his mask, breathing harshly, he moved toward the recent additions to his collection. Among them were two stuffed bears, one male, and the other female. He arranged them in a lewd position and started to masturbate. As he stroked himself, he remembered Haden and Daphne. How young they were. How desperate to be apart.

As he came, spraying the bears with his semen, he reflected how for Haden and Daphne, the scars of that evening in the motel would never heal. The place was redolent with loss, sadness and pain.

The Curator couldn't imagine a better place if he tried.

FUCK SHOCK

When it was over and he lay on the floor of his apartment with the taste of her on his tongue, Robert Duffy was convinced he would never have another satisfying sexual experience for as long as he lived.

Sprawled on the carpet, looking like the subject of a chalk drawing at a crime scene, Robert reached into his sweaty underwear and gripped his cock. It slithered and slipped in his palm, still moist with her fluids. Slowly, his wrist began to work, pumping up and down. His brow popped fresh beads of sweat. The heat radiated off his flesh in a reeking pall. He pumped harder. Then stopped. Opening his palm, he stared at his limp cock. It refused to comply with his need for release. Standing, he walked into the bedroom, crawled under the unmade, unwashed sheets and eventually, after another fruitless attempt at pleasure, slipped into a restless sleep.

His sexual frustration persisted for several weeks. An urge was building inside of Robert, filling him, until his nights were robbed of sleep and his stomach shrank inside of him. The thought of her only compounded the problem. Every time he caught a glimpse of his naked reflection, be it the sunken chest with its nest of dark, wiry hair, or the shapeless contour of his ass, her shadow seemed to slither across his skin like a retinal afterimage. Her memory traced snail-trails across the map of his flesh, and with every gaze, Robert's mind reflected ecstatically upon the encounter that had forever changed him. He would shiver, his skin prickling with gooseflesh. Soon it was coated in a scrim of sweat, as if his whole body had transmuted into a sexual organ, sheened in pre-seminal fluid in anticipation of the act. Only then was he able to sprout an erection. It was feeble at best, but the important thing was that Robert's blood flowed true, and he suspected that her venom was partly responsible for this. But as soon as he tried to pleasure himself, the shadow-memory lost substance, and his cock fell limp in his hand.

Reflecting on this later, as he lounged dejectedly in an old sofa chair he salvaged from the roadside, Robert realized that he was suffering from a legitimate case of fuck shock. Not to be compared with its cousin, shell shock, fuck shock was the rare and unfortunate product of the most satisfying sexual encounter one could ever experience. The result was a chronic dissatisfaction with any lesser forms of sexual pleasure. In short, the victim of fuck shock could never be satisfied until he found an experience that transcended the one that brought on the affliction in the first place. Robert doubted this very much because when he tried to find her again at the abandoned storefront, the building was gone, replaced by a newly paved parking lot. Desperate now, Robert tried to find fulfillment in other ways.

He opened his laptop and searched for escort services in the region. The most promising result was a small business called Bijou that offered a variety of women ranging in age and ethnicity. Fortunately, the place allowed for booking to be made by text message, allowing Robert the ease of privacy. He decided on a twenty-two-year-old brunette named Endora. He quickly received a response by text stating that she was available for outcalls and would arrive at his home shortly.

When she rang twenty minutes later he buzzed her in. Opening the door, he saw the woman advertised on the website only now, unlike her digital counterpart, she had a face. A weary complexion puckered the thin, pink skin around her eyes, which were a muted shade of blue. Her nose was large and pitted with blackheads, distorting the otherwise symmetrical quality of her face. When she smiled, Robert saw that her teeth were stained nicotine yellow.

But as Robert's eyes roved over her face, he realized that they shared a mutual disappointment for each other. The ingeniousness of her smile was betrayed in the small tremors at the corners of her mouth.

Robert looked down at himself, his dirty shirt, jogging pants, and unkempt hair and said, "I was going to wait for you to get here before I showered, just so you know that I'm clean."

She nodded politely. "That's very considerate of you."

Walking toward the bathroom to shower for the first time in perhaps a week, Robert pointed at the rescued sofa chair and said, "You can sit there and relax. I won't be long."

When he emerged from the shower, a towel wrapped around his emaciated waist, he found Endora sitting on his bed, smoothing out the wrinkles with her manicured hands. Her lips, greased in black, parted wetly and she said, "What are you thinking?"

Robert sat down beside her, shoulder to shoulder. He had shaved the week's worth of stubble from his face to make the encounter more tolerable for the whore. He smelled thickly of foam and aftershave.

"I like to be surprised," Robert said, and then, summoning the phrase from the storehouses of memory, "Show me a new experience."

Endora smiled politely. Robert wasn't the first weirdo she had encountered. One guy, tall and well groomed had sobbed during sex and afterwards emptied the sodden condom in the sink and then filled it with water to check for leaks.

But Robert was different from the usual john. Something haunted him; she could see it in his eyes, the movements of his body. A specter enveloped him, an aura hovering inches above the skin like heat baking off asphalt.

Endora touched his chest, twining her fingers through his hair. She did not detect the usual thrill of anticipation that affected the other johns. She might as well have been touching a corpse, still warm and in the grip of a bizarre half-life. He did not thrill to her touch. He might not have even felt it. For him, it was nothing but skin against skin, as cold and sexless as a physician's probing hands. The soggy towel was quickly discarded, adding to the already mountainous heap of soiled clothing on the floor. Endora gently guided Robert onto his back with a palm pressed flat against his chest. He lowered, fanning out his arms, his knees bent over the edge of the bed and his toes pointed toward the floor. Endora shed her clothing like a loose second skin, and added it to the floor heap. She was slightly broader in the shoulders than what might be considered beautiful. Her breasts, likewise, were far apart, but full and natural, the nipples bristling with small bumps. As she took him inside her, Robert's mind drifted far away, guided by the memory of her. The venom stirred in his veins.

———

He met her at a sex club in the basement of an abandoned store-front. The wall-length windows were plastered on the inside with a mosaic of yellowing newspaper. He knocked on the door twice and was greeted by a woman in her mid-twenties with a bun fastened tightly to the back of her head.

"You must be Robert. Please come in."

Robert had recently broken up with his girlfriend of two years, with the pretext of meeting, but more specifically, fucking other people. Their relationship had grown stale, the sex predictable and routine. Now Robert was a free man and the myriad possibilities danced inside his mind whenever he sat alone in his apartment. One night, indulging in the depravity of his imagination, he decided to meet a woman and have sex with her. It was, he resolved, the best way to snuff out his boredom. His planning was swift and pragmatic. He didn't know any women who would sleep with him if he sent out a request by phone or text. So Robert turned to the only available alternative, the Internet. He opened the browser and searched for adult classified in his area. He scrolled through various listings, through pictures of women, clad in skimpy nightwear, with their heads cropped off, and homo-sexual men exploiting their swollen pride. Then, halfway through the fourth page, Robert spied a listing for an establishment that offered unusual sexual services at a discounted price.

It was this advertisement that brought him to the abandoned storefront and the woman with the bun. He stood in a vast, dark space with empty shelves lining the stained tile floors. The woman led him to the very end of the room, through a curtain down wooden stairs.

Robert found himself at the beginning of a long hallway lined with paintings. Each of them hung at waist level. The woman took him by the hand and guided him down the passage. One of the paintings was an unskillful portrait of a clown done by John Wayne Gacy, with a glory hole where its mouth should have been. From behind the painting came a muffled weeping sound and Robert shivered to think what crouched there.

Then, all at once, the lights sputtered and went out, plunging the hallway into darkness. Robert stopped and the whole world seemed to follow. Robbed of his sight, the only things his senses could register was the woman's soft grip on his hand, and the skin prickling moans behind the painting. Then the woman's voice rose out of the void, "Don't move. Hold your breath."

Robert's heart was hammering in his chest. He did as he was told. It happened very quickly. The lights flickered on an off in quick succession, partly revealing meaty, dripping things shrieking in the dark. They moved across the ceiling on sinewy arms or tentacles, passing directly over Robert's head, four or five of them —he couldn't tell for sure—screaming like women in labor. Then the lights returned, and the creatures were gone.

Robert turned and looked at the woman with fear in his eyes, and she squeezed his hand, managing somehow to dismiss the horror with the pressure of her touch.

"Nothing will hurt you here," she said.

At last, they entered a doorway at the end of the hall. It opened into a whitewash room with a bulb suspended from frayed wire. In the center of the room was a bare mattress stained in various shades of red and yellow. The woman told Robert to remove his clothing and lie down. As Robert unbuttoned his shirt and lowered his jeans he had the strange sensation of becoming aware in the midst of a dream. But it quickly faded as he lowered his bare ass on to the mattress. The woman got naked and sat down opposite him with her legs spread. Her genitals were neatly shaved, but it didn't take Robert long to notice the strange scar encircling her vulva. He reached out to touch her, but she gently pushed his hand away.

"Watch," she said, looking down.

The scar around her vulva shifted until the genitals bulged outward. A set of spidery legs the same color and texture as her skin twitched and finally extracted themselves from a series of pink grooves on her abdomen and thighs. They were attached to the vulva itself, which functioned independently of the woman's body. Once it had detached itself from the woman, leaving a dark pink crater, it crawled down her thigh toward Robert, whose first instinct was to cower away.

"Don't be afraid," the woman said. "She will show you a new experience."

Slowly, Robert started to relax. The creature crawled up his leg and loomed over his crotch. Its mouth shuddered, disgorging a stream of whitish mucus before a worm slithered out onto Robert's genitals. Its glistening grey skin was porous and covered in ridges. Hundreds of tiny legs undulated as it moved.

It took Robert in its mouth. There was a brief moment of pain and then a rush of euphoria unlike any Robert had experienced before.

"It's her venom," the woman said, as Robert's eyes rolled back and a moan escaped his lips. "Just relax."

The worm shuddered, its body expanding and contracting, bringing Robert closer to orgasm. The pleasure was so intense a rivulet of saliva escaped the corner of his mouth and traced a shimmering line along his jaw. His body shuddered. His veins filled alternately with fire and ice water. The worm pumped, dripping slime that matted Robert's pubic hair. Then, all at once, his arms flew out. He collapsed prone on the mattress. His balls tightened against his perineum as he came. Semen oozed out of the worm's pores and coursed down its spongy flesh in a series of pearly stripes.

When it was over, the worm removed itself from Robert like a sock pulled inside out. Regaining its shape, it crawled up his chest, trailing a mixture of slime and semen. Robert could feel its tiny legs tickling his neck as it slithered up his chin. Its mouth, warm, wet and puckered like an anus pressed against his lips. He tasted himself along with the raw liverish tang of the worm.

She was utterly beautiful, the conqueror worm that would forever haunt the ruin of his sexual existence.

———

Robert opened his eyes and saw Endora staring down at him. "What's the matter with you?" she said, climbing off. He was flaccid and unable to perform. Robert ignored her and stared at the textured ceiling. There he saw a series of patterns like worms eager to bestow new sexual experiences. Pleasure, he knew, had reached its summit. And so, with the taste of her a ghost on his tongue, Robert decided to become her priest, to worship her memory even into darkness.

THE BLACK WATERS OF BABYLON

When Philip Vorstadt arrived at the Seaside Rehabilitation Center, his body was broken, his mind on the brink of collapse.

The facility jutted from a rock cliff, its outermost wall suspended over the waves rolling and thundering below. Its sterile concrete exterior was splashed and bleached by sea spray, the windows girding its length tinted black and opaque. The main body of the facility was capped by a secondary structure that rose more than fifty feet into the air, a massive stone finger pointing at the sky. It appeared to serve no practical purpose and stood out in stark contrast against the heavy black clouds marshaled across the horizon.

A flight of stairs carved out of the rock ascended to Chinese-style double doors inlaid with brass gilding and painted a dark emerald green. Two men wearing hybrid outfits—part formal suit, park workman's uniform—of the same hue as the door behind them, stood guard. Their faces were entirely covered by helmets equipped with dark, reflective glasses and some kind of tubing that extended from the mouth area to the back of the head. They stood completely still, hands folded over their abdomens.

Vorstadt had not taken the stairs because of his confinement to a wheelchair, but instead rode an elevator encased in glass up to the main entrance. When he reached the top, he turned his head slowly to one side, grimacing at the pain sizzling like an old dyna-mite fuse down his neck and back, and stared out at the landscape fronting the rehab center.

Emptiness. Nothing but emptiness for miles and miles to the ends of the earth. At some point, the rocky terrain gave way to cracked soil studded with cottongrass, but otherwise Vorstadt perceived no other signs of life. Not a single seabird glided below the belly of the clouds, nor could a lone patient or doctor be seen taking a stroll to break the day's tedium. The facility and its envi-rons were a drab purgatorial waiting room, a middle ground between shattered hopes and new beginnings.

Vorstadt had exhausted all other options, and only this desolate sanctuary remained. Doctors hundreds of miles away in the "other world" as Vorstadt had already come to know the place of his birth and residence, deemed his injuries irreparable. They had conducted various treatments and surgeries without any success. All Vorstadt was left with was a patchwork of thick, knotted scars and a debilitating twitch in his left eye as a result of post-surgical nerve damage. Granted, his injuries were extensive, but taking into account the recent advances in medical science and technology, Vorstadt thought it absurd that absolutely nothing could be done to improve his condition. As it was, his entire body was racked by perpetual agony. He could barely eat or drink on his own, let alone attend to his own toilet, and his speech—though he was rarely inclined to speak—tumbled past his broken teeth like hard chunks of vomit. The resulting sound was wet and nearly incompre-hensible.

It all came down to this. The rehab center would either provide him with the healing he needed, or he would kill himself. He had even planned the method of his destruction. Seeing that he couldn't properly grasp a weapon between his fingers, he managed to convince his partner, Darren, who was skilled in computers and robotics, to engineer an execution device. Darren flat out refused to kill Vorstadt with his own hands. Instead, he rigged the shotgun he would have otherwise employed in the assisted suicide to a simple contraption that responded to Vorstadt's voice command. The intention was for Vorstadt to position his face directly in front of the barrel and speak the word "flower," which he could pronounce with little difficulty. The computer wired to the contraption would prompt a makeshift finger curled around the trigger to retract and discharge the shotgun, scattering Vorstadt's thoughts and memories in a spray of bloody bone. It was an elaborate and admittedly silly way to go, but prior to his infirmity, Vorstadt was something of a showman, easily able to capture the headlines as he ran his business with dramatic flair. So, to those who knew him best, his chosen method of destruction was very much within character.

"How are we feeling, Mr. Vorstadt?" asked the nurse who had been charged with pushing his wheelchair since he arrived at the center.

She was short statured and sturdily built, the sleeves of her olive uniform hemmed to reveal the lumps of muscle on her arms. Her hair was purple and combed flat toward the crown of her head. A pale curlicue of discolored skin in the shape of a snake— likely a manifestation of vitiligo—sketched itself around her left eye and across her forehead. When she smiled, Vorstadt noticed teeth capped with gunmetal fillings.

In response to her question, Vorstadt returned a clumsy nod. He was feeling fine. Not very optimistic or nervous, just fine. He had long since tempered his expectations, even though the rehab center came highly recommended in the more affluent circles he frequented. Many of his colleagues and acquaintances had paid ridiculous sums of money to treat their gout, back pain or arthritis. One guy even claimed to have been cured of erectile dysfunction. Had these been the only anecdotes associated with the facility, Vorstadt would have dismissed the place entirely, but there was another point of interest for him.

Her name was Mia. Six months ago, shortly before Vorstadt sustained his own injuries, Mia's now ex-husband had beaten her to the point where she was no longer able to walk. Vorstadt had seen her condition in the aftermath of the assault, a dispirited wreck, and it had hit him hard. Which made it all the more shocking when he saw her again after she had returned from the facility, her scars healed, her gait more graceful than ever. Vorstadt could only conceive of the change in the most cliché of terms. It was nothing short of a miracle.

Even having seen what the facility could do, Vorstadt was still cautious to hope. Whenever he closed his eyes, he saw the barrel of the shotgun pointed at him, seductive as a lover's bedroom gaze.

The doors to the facility opened with a whir of mechanical gears. Out stepped a tall woman in a sleek black suit with a jacket so long it trailed at her heels like a cape. She was shaved bald, accentuating the startling beauty of her slanted chestnut eyes. Approaching Vorstadt she bowed low and said, "It is a pleasure to meet you, Mr. Vorstadt. I am Director Maikawa, the heart that pumps blood through this facility."

Vorstadt nodded again.

"If you will join me," Maikawa said, gesturing to the innards of the rehab center. "We shall begin your treatment right away."

The nurse pushed Vorstadt over the threshold, the slight rise of the transition strip jostling his body from one arm of the chair to the other. He vaguely felt drool escape his mouth, but could do nothing about it. Vorstadt was used to such indignities. To avoid frustration he focused on his surroundings instead. The first thing he noticed about the facility was the smell. It was a rotten odor, sickly sweet, like spoiled fruit with a fishy undertone mixed with the lulling perfume of lavender.

Whitewash walls, echoing ivory floors, grey tone artwork. The place seemed empty. Vorstadt didn't see anyone else on his way down the central hall, past rows of steel doors and open rooms neatly arranged with Oriental furniture. It was as though he were the only patient, or else the others were deliberately kept from his view to maintain the illusion that he was receiving the facility's utmost care and attention.

"We studied your infirmities at length," Maikawa said, breaking the almost hypnotic tedium of their echoing footsteps, "and believe that you will only benefit from our most intensive treatment. Tell me, Mr. Vorstadt, have you ever undergone hydrotherapy?"

"N-no," he managed to say.

"As its name suggests, it is a form of alternative medicine that uses water to treat various physical ailments. Outside this facility, it is used in a rather *benign* fashion," she lingered on the word, savored it, "usually through pool exercise or floating therapy. Here, we do things a little differently."

They reached the end of the hallway, where a set of glass doors led into darkness. Vorstadt could hear a faint wind howling behind them, strangely amplified as though the sound were whooshing through a tunnel. He realized then they must have been standing where the massive stone pillar rose out of the middle of the facility. The pillar was open to the sky, which explained the mournful bellow of the wind. What purpose could it serve, he wondered. He was confident he would soon find out.

Maikawa turned to face him. "Through these doors is the pride of our facility, the Rod of Babylon. It extends seventy-five feet into the air, and tunnels through the rock beneath us, to the cold, black waters below. It is there we intend to heal you."

She held out her hand toward him in a demonstrative gesture. Vorstadt followed the movement with his eyes and noticed, for the first time, the perfect grid of puncture wounds on her palm. Each hole was bright red with coagulated blood, the skin around them white as a fish's belly. When she noticed his gaze, Maikawa smiled modestly and slowly drew her fingers into a fist.

The sight left Vorstadt with a queasy feeling in the pit of his stomach. It didn't appear to be any injury he was familiar with; it was too perfect, too clean. And not to mention a trypophobe's worst nightmare. Before he could consider the matter further, he was struck by a blast of sea wind.

Director Maikawa opened the glass doors and invited Vorstadt inside. The nurse pushed him forward and the overhead lights sputtered into activity. The sudden brightness stung Vorstadt's eyes. They were gathered in a small antechamber lined with steel and reinforced with concrete. A series of vents along the far wall admitted the outside air. Every surface shined and gave back a distorted reflection. The place was bare except for a solitary locker in the corner and a canvas harness attached to some kind of pulley mechanism facing yet another door.

"Nurse, if you will please remove Mr. Vorstadt's clothing."

The nurse engaged the wheelchair's manual brake, walked

around to face Vorstadt, who nodded his consent, and proceeded to undress him. He hated every moment of it. She was much gentler than his homecare nurse, he would give her that, but the whole process was no less undignified or embarrassing. He hated how she needed to guide his limbs into a more comfortable position as soon as she removed them from a shirtsleeve or pant leg; hated the feeling of her breath fanning his skin as she toiled at the task; hated the way his naked body looked under fluorescent lights, all pallor and sagging, atrophied muscles. He fixed her with his gaze and mumbled, "This had better goddamn work."

"We will do our best, Mr. Vorstadt," she answered with a gunmetal smile.

She wheeled his bare, pathetic form toward the harness and strapped him in, the coarse canvas looping around his biceps, thighs, chest, and buttocks to ensure maximum support. Vorstadt now realized that the harness could be raised or lowered, presumably down the shaft on the opposite side of the door, with the help of the pulley system. For the second time today, a queasy pang lanced through the pit of his stomach.

The nurse produced a keycard from her pocket and swiped it through a reader on the door. It beeped, disengaging the lock, and the nurse moved to open it. Vorstadt was assaulted once more by a surge of briny air, only this time it was strong enough to make him flinch. The spray dappled his face and sent gooseflesh skittering down his spine. When the initial blast of air had subsided and Vorstadt was able to open his eyes fully, he saw framed in the doorway a darkness so thick, it was more an absence of matter than light.

Wasn't the Rod of Babylon open to the sky? How else could the breeze find its way into the antechamber? And more importantly, wouldn't the drab daylight filter down? Why, or more precisely, how could this utter blackness be possible?

A headache started to pulse at the base of his skull. He averted his gaze, looking up at Maikawa, who said, "You will be lowered into the pool beneath the facility. Treatment will take anywhere between four and eight hours. When enough time has elapsed we will examine your condition and proceed with additional treatment if needed. Please be aware that once you have been lowered into the pool, you will have no way of communicating with us. Treatment cannot be interrupted if you expect to see results. Do you understand?"

Vorstadt's mind was a maelstrom of conflicting emotions—confusion, fear, doubt and wonder—all vying for dominance, but none of them winning, and so he was left in a state of total bewilderment. All he could muster was a weak nod.

"Very well," Maikawa said.

A quick glance at the nurse and Vorstadt was lifted out of his chair and into the nurse's arms. She carried him to the threshold and lowered him into a sitting position, with his legs dangling over the edge of the abyss. Looking down, Vorstadt saw that the darkness cut his legs off at the knees. He blinked the illusion away.

"We will see you in a few hours. Godspeed, Mr. Vorstadt," said Maikawa.

From behind him came the grinding of old machinery. Then the nurse nudged him over the precipice, into the devouring dark.

He didn't know how long he was suspended, weightless, in that void. Time was useless, an artifact of the lighted world Vorstadt feared he would never see again. His ears were filled with the mournful cries of the wind. Sea spray kissed his naked flesh and set him shivering. He smelled the sea, the rotting stench of exposed algae, and the occasional whiff of fish guts.

Vorstadt closed his eyes and thought about Darren. He remembered his lover's reaction upon stepping into the critical care unit. If only his mind hadn't chosen consciousness at that precise moment. Never before had he seen a face transform so dramatically. The sheer horror and heartbreak that pulled Darren's formerly slack features apart was surreal as a cheap prosthetic effect. Vorstadt would never have thought, never dreamed, that Darren's facial muscles were capable of such a sickening distortion. Unable to move due to being so tightly bandaged, Vorstadt could do nothing but stare, realizing in that moment that his pain was not exclusively his own. Darren, whom he loved more than anything, shared it too. Which meant that his sojourn at the clinic wasn't a selfish pursuit. Darren would be undergoing the same treatment by proxy.

The image of the execution device returned again to Vorstadt's mind. It occurred to him that should the treatment fail and the shotgun empty its load into his skull, he would be confronted one last time by Darren's horrified expression before plunging into death—his own brief moment of hell.

Cold, black water engulfed his toes. Vorstadt jerked violently, the movement sending a cataclysm of pain through his entire body. The water crept up his legs, washed over his thighs and swallowed his midsection. The pulley mechanism halted just as the sea lapped against his chin. Vorstadt let out a deep, startled breath. It was lost in the roar of the wind.

The long wait began.

He kept his eyes closed, cleared his mind, and tried to relax. Eventually the wind receded to white noise and he lost all sensation below the neckline. He was a disembodied head floating in space.

Doubt frequently tried to force itself into his mind—how can this possibly work? It's a scam. There's no hope you—but Vorstadt was easily able to push it back. He entered into a state of deep relaxation, becoming one with the water, a liquid being who swayed to the rhythm of the ocean. It entered into his awareness in the same way a truth is known in a dream, that he was suspended over a trench several miles deep. The emptiness impressed itself on his brain, provoking feelings of reverence and wonder. He remained in this state of sublime gnosis for what seemed like hours then, over the noise of the wind, began to hear a faint music from somewhere below.

It was unlike any music he had heard before, and could only be distinguished as such because it had a melody. Slowly it grew louder and more distinct as whatever made it approached the surface. At first Vorstadt thought he was imagining the whole thing, but when something heavy brushed against his leg and the music swelled to a crescendo, he realized it was all too real. Whatever it was moved with fluid grace, its fleshy net-like body fanning his calves. Long strands of hair coiled around his toes.

He kicked in vain, his nerves flaring with agony, but the thing maintained its orbit around him. The music was almost deafening now. He lifted his head to the invisible sky and screamed. At that moment, a stinger pierced the sole of his foot and flooded his bloodstream with warmth. His scream subsided into a drooling moan. Abruptly the music stopped and the wind resumed its howling dominance.

Winter receded into spring and then early summer. Vorstadt took advantage of the weather and decided to take lunch outside the office. The sidewalk was beautifully firm under his feet. He stuffed his hands deep into his pockets and walked fast, feeling the sultry breeze palm and caress his face.

At the café, he ordered a coffee and sandwich. As he extended a handful of coins across the counter, he noticed the cashier staring at the patch of discolored skin across his knuckles. It looked like an early manifestation of vitiligo. He smiled at her, completed the transaction and stepped out into the street.

His phone buzzed. It was Darren.

"Will you be home tonight?"

"Yeah. Why? Do you have something in mind?"

"Not exactly," he said. "I just want to see you. Ever since you recovered you can't seem to sit down for longer than five minutes. You're always busy doing something."

"I'll be there. In fact, if you want—"

A sharp, searing pain tore across his thigh and then the side-walk was rushing up to meet him. He managed to break his fall with an outstretched hand, and as soon as he recovered, moved into a sitting position with his knees drawn up to his chest. A bicycle lay on its side several feet away, the rider in the process of getting to his feet.

"I'm so sorry, man," the cyclist was saying. "Are you okay?"

Vorstadt glanced down at the tear in his dress pants, the ragged edges dark with blood.

"I'll be fine," he said and allowed the biker to help him to his feet.

In the office bathroom, Vorstadt locked himself in a stall, unhooked his belt, and carefully shimmied out of his pants. The cut was at least an inch deep, but it had already stopped bleeding. He sat on the lid of the toilet seat and, using the pointer finger of both hands, pried open the laceration to examine it more closely. His mouth went dry.

Instead of muscle, fat and bone, the inside of his thigh was filled with rows of short, nubby teeth. When he prodded one of them with his finger, it retreated deeper into his body like a startled worm. In its place came a gush of yellowish brown fluid reeking of dead fish, and a black fingerling that landed on the bathroom tile and started thrashing around. Its skin was featureless and slick, lamplight eyes glowed with bioluminescence above a set of human-like teeth. Vorstadt calmly crushed it under his heel. He wasn't alarmed. This was the price of his treatment, the only way he could have avoided the kiss of the shotgun.

He opened the cut wider, hissing through gnashed teeth. A fish's eye became visible at the bottom of the wound and rolled to look at him. The pupil was large and inquisitive. He stared back, impassive, then yanked his hands away as the wound clamped shut like a mouth. The skin knitted itself back together, leaving behind a strip of bleached, colorless skin.

Vorstadt stood up and pulled up his pants, making a mental note to have them mended if possible. He turned and stared into the toilet bowl, its waters calm and sending back a mirror's clear reflection. Movement deep inside his thigh made his leg twitch. They were getting restless. Soon the full price of his miracle would have to be paid. The flood was coming.

STAG LOOP

Amanda found the film in the discount bin at the adult video store. The case insert was missing. Only a pale strip of masking tape scrawled with the words "stag loop" served to identify its contents. She bought it for three dollars, along with a handful of more legitimate-looking DVDs, as a gift for her boyfriend, Logan.

When she returned home, the sharp, icy fingers of winter had dragged the sun into an early grave. The house was muted in shadow; the only sound the rumble of Logan's snoring upstairs. Amanda followed it to the bedroom. Nyx was curled up at the foot of the mattress, purring ecstatically, and regarded Amanda with her golden-green eyes. Amanda scooped the animal in her arms, turned to face the cheval mirror behind the door, and studied her reflection.

Enough moonlight crept through a slit in the curtains to sketch out one side of her body. The result looked something like a work of scratch art: fine strokes of silver against solid black. Nyx appeared to grow out of her chest, the jagged tracery of her pelt gleaming like polished steel.

"Look at those beautiful ladies," Amanda said and kissed the cat between the ears.

She replaced Nyx on the bed, searched the grocery bag of DVDs, pulled out the one marked "stag loop", and slotted it into the player. Logan stirred. Amanda checked her watch. He was supposed to leave any minute for the graveyard shift.

She crawled up beside him and breathed hot breath in his ear.

"Time to swim up out of those dreams," she whispered.

Her eyes swished to the television. The film was starting. The white flicker of damaged negative was replaced by a lingering shot of a sixties-era living room. The picture was yellowed in sepia and poorly lit. Amanda knew right away that it was a bad VHS transfer. The living room was furnished with a couch, garishly floral-patterned, a coffee table with a white porcelain bowl in the middle of it, and an ugly Grecian urn off to one corner.

A man with shoulder-length hair entered the frame. He waved impatiently to someone off-camera. After a beat, the actress stumbled into the scene. Her hair was styled in a bob that framed her face in an inverted triangle. She wore a button-up dress and no bra. Her breasts curved under the sheer fabric. Timidly, she approached her co-star and allowed him to undress her. After a mediocre blowjob—Amanda realized that vintage porn was closer to real life than the modern fare—they fucked on the couch. The scratchy background noises gave way to porn groove.

Amanda let out a soft chuckle and recalled her attention to Logan. He groaned, threw an arm over his face, and Amanda rolled back the sheets to expose him to the night air. He was naked except for a pair of boxer briefs. His morning wood was more than a suggestion under the membrane of cotton.

"What are you doing?" he said, voice drunk with sleep.

Amanda kissed him on the stomach. His skin was hard and soft, the light smattering of hair tickling her lips. She moved up to his chest, planting little kisses along the way. He made a noise halfway between a grunt and a moan. His arm slid away from his face and their lips met. They kissed gently at first, Logan still only half awake, and then grew more urgent, passionate. His breath was stale, but it did little to deter Amanda's affections. Over the lip smacking and panting, the stag loop provided a comedic backdrop to their activities.

Soon the music reached Logan's ears, piercing the blinders of his arousal. He laughed, a loud bark that sent vibrations down his stomach.

"What is this shit?" he said, staring beyond her at the television.

Amanda pulled away, lips plump and sheened in saliva, and followed his gaze. Onscreen, the woman had mounted the man in the cowgirl position, with her back facing the camera. She bounced up and down, throwing her head around in exaggerated paroxysms of pleasure. With a species of envy, Amanda noticed the beauty of the woman's back. Her shoulder blades stood out in sharp relief, softly pointed, sliding under the buttermilk skin with each thrust of her pelvis. A beauty mark fringed the slope of her right back dimple. At first Amanda thought it was a discrepancy in the image, a scar on the negative, but then it moved in conjunction with the woman's flesh, startlingly black in that sepia world.

"This porn is ancient," Logan said. "Where did you find it?"

"The adult store," Amanda said, eyes lingering on the screen. "Don't worry it wasn't expensive."

"I was going to say. Amateur porn filmed in the dark looks better than this. This is just weird… and creepy."

"Because it's old?"

Logan gestured toward the screen. "It looks *off.*"

"What are you talking about?" Amanda propped her head in her hands. "It's two average-looking people having sex. He doesn't have an obscenely large dick, and her tits aren't big enough to smother a grown man. They're normal."

Logan shrugged. "It's not that. I can't put my finger on it. Maybe it's the yellow tint or the shitty lighting. It makes their eyes, her eyes especially, look empty."

"Maybe she was doped up on something."

"Could be. This was the decade of peace and love, after all."

Amanda playfully flicked Logan's cock. He flinched. "Well I think she's beautiful."

"For a ghost, maybe."

"Why would you say that?"

Logan wagged a knowing finger. "I think I figured it out. The girl doesn't look real, but more like a cheap optical effect than actual flesh and blood."

Amanda grinned. "You're thinking way too hard about this. It's a fucking porno."

Logan sighed. "Yeah, you're right." Then in a sleazy accent, said, "So how's about we bring our own porno to its natural conclusion?"

Amanda said nothing, only lowered herself back down on Logan, filling the room once again with sounds of their passion.

Meanwhile, on the television, the longhaired man came on his co-star's chest. The picture sputtered to black, to be followed by the second scene in the loop. It was dark, grey-tones. Two men and one woman were writhing on a bedspread veined with wrinkles. A distorted, porn-groove rendition of a church hymn played in the background. As the larger of the two men penetrated the woman from behind, Amanda and Logan were already naked and moving together between disheveled and twisted sheets.

———

After Logan left for work, Amanda found herself once again in front of the cheval mirror. The porn loop continued to play in the background, spewing a funky version of honkytonk piano. Amanda frowned at her shadowed reflection, pulled her lips apart in a grimace.

While alone, Amanda found amusement in affecting different personalities. Now she was testing her capacity to be a bitch. She loved Logan more than anything, but even so, and purely out of curiosity, she held an inner dialogue between the two of them, merely to taste an alternate side of her personality.

In this mental staging, Logan woke from his nap and tried pulling her into an embrace, but she denied him, icily retreating from his touch. Your breath stinks, this version of her said, you have to get to work. But, Logan stammered, a child denied his favorite sweets, we still have time, come on. He looked at the clock by way of evidence. You have a hand, Amanda said sharply, use it.

The real Amanda, head bowed and gazing into the mirror from beneath the hood of her eyes, laughed. She didn't usually have to resort to such caustic remarks, but the potential for verbal violence was definitely inside her. Slumbering. Everyone held an aptitude for darkness, Amanda thought. Better to explore it in her mind, watching the shadows play across her face in the mirror, than exercise it in real life. It was much safer that way, more benign.

Do and say what you can safely to others, and save the rest for the imagination. That was the essence of Amanda's philosophy. This principle allowed her, even for a moment, to become someone else. You may only live once, she mused, but who's stopping you from trying on different personalities?

The woman from the stag loop materialized in her mind's eye. Amanda wondered what she was like, what kind of personality inhabited that beautiful body. She seemed shy, but that was probably just an act similar to what Amanda routinely affected in the mirror. If that was the case, then who was the woman lurking under that veneer? Amanda disengaged herself from the mirror's gaze and rewound the stag loop to the first scene. She let it play for a moment then paused the picture at a frame where the woman *almost* seemed to look into the camera.

Logan was right, there was something weird about her eyes. They stared right through you—empty. She shivered. Keeping the video on pause, Amanda left the room to use the bathroom. Nyx followed.

Amanda watched television in the den until midnight. She alternated between the usual reality and variety programs while Nyx slept on her lap. When she finally mounted the steps back to her bedroom, tired enough for sleep, she saw the porn actress' face frozen on the screen, and realized she'd forgotten to turn off the television. The actress continued to stare with that same emptiness, crystalized in a lurid moment decades past.

Instead of ejecting the DVD, Amanda sat at the foot of the bed, hands clasping her knees, and tried to see beyond the cluster of pixels to the identity buried underneath. She yearned, with a sudden intensity, to know this woman on a deep, fundamental level. She wanted to appropriate her character, taste the exoticism of a porn star of the golden age. Only this time, she didn't want to simply imagine it, as her role-play had compelled her to do, but instead wanted something more, something tangible. To slide into her sheath of skin, wear it like a second-hand sweater, inhale its foreign scent, taste the strange sweat squeezing from its pores.

Amanda shook herself out of the reverie. What strange thoughts, she mused with a smile. She supposed they were born out of boredom. Lately, her days were fixed in the rigidity of routine—waking up early, working from nine to five at the insurance firm, eating a boxed dinner in front of the TV, then bed—and even something as mundane as a vintage porn loop could spur her on an imaginative journey. Private role-play to kept her entertained during life's boring moments. It was an unconventional hobby, but Amanda wasn't exactly one to take up knitting or scrapbooking, and she liked the thrill it ignited in her belly. She turned off the television and crawled under the covers. The sheets still smelled strongly of Logan, the musk of his body and the slightly cloying aroma of his cologne. She extinguished the bedside lamp and closed her eyes.

In the theatre of her mind the porn loop continued to play, feeding her further exhibitions of carnal pleasure. Her imagination became a tableau of sex acts—a series of lantern slides depicting countless variations of fellatio, cunningulus, intercourse, and sodomy—all of it eerily bathed in a yellow glow. As she drifted closer to the well of sleep, she began seeing flashes of the woman's eyes. I wonder what else is on the loop, Amanda thought as she sunk into sleep's warm, black waters.

She woke two hours later with the distinct feeling that Logan was sleeping beside her. Rolling to face him, she muttered something about his breath stinking and fell back asleep.

Her dream was the yellow of jaundice. The camera of her subconscious was fixed on the floral pattern sofa from the porn loop. A ball of lint, tethered to a strand of black hair, wavered in an unknown breeze. Then the camera focused, the image closing in on the crevice between the back of the couch and the cushions. Amanda was carried into a darkness fringed with loose strands of needlework. It felt as though she were descending into a pit in the middle of a lightless jungle. For some time she incubated in darkness, becoming one with it, it becoming one with her, before a pinprick of light appeared, drawing her attention. Amanda swam toward it.

She found herself under studio lights, in a sixties-era living room. A negligee was draped carelessly over her body, one shoulder suggestively exposed. The woman with the spectral eyes was sitting on the couch. She said, "Care to join me?"

Her hand went out, the nails long and manicured. Amanda felt a measure of reluctance tug at her brain. She stayed rooted to the spot.

"Don't you want to see?" the woman asked. "To feel what it's like inside?"

Amanda opened her mouth to speak, but no sound emerged.

"Just sit beside me. We can take it slow," the woman went on.

A flash of lucidity and Amanda realized this was nothing more than a dream. She was in the playground of her imagination, where anything goes. No choices she made, for good or ill, had the power to affect her in the waking world. She could throw herself off a bridge to feel her stomach lurch into her throat, or cheat on Logan with one of the reality stars she'd gawked at before bed. None of it mattered. Dreaming gave her a free pass to do whatever the hell she wanted. Amanda took a step toward the woman and...

Her eyes snapped open. The bedroom was a uniform blackness. Amanda couldn't distinguish the objects and furniture scattered throughout it. She blinked, hoping her vision would adjust, but a veil had been pressed over her eyes. Distantly, in another part of the house, she heard Nyx meowing, a low, threatened note. The clock in the kitchen ticked off the seconds, sharp and clear in the dark. A floorboard creaked, probably the house settling. Amanda stretched out an arm, hand passing over the space belonging to Logan. It was warm and shallowly indented. The air smelt vaguely of sour breath. Nyx let out a sharp yowl. All these sensations felt incredibly dreamlike.

Comforted by this realization, Amanda submitted herself once again to sleep.

———

She was sitting beside the woman now.

Something shrieked far off, the distorted cry of an animal in pain. Amanda placed her hand on the woman's thigh. It was warm and downy, like something freshly born.

"You're very beautiful," Amanda said, tracing her fingers across the woman's nubile flesh.

Their eyes met, the woman's lazy with seduction, and Amanda felt herself being drawn into their emptiness.

"I've been here too long," the woman said. "I'm happy for your company.

She clasped Amanda's hand in her own.

"What happens now?" Amanda said.

A mixture of fear and excitement coursed through her veins. She knew on a level of dream logic that she was about to participate in the ultimate role-play.

"I invite you inside," the woman said, with a flourish of her manicured nails. "All I need is your consent."

"Can you show me what will happen before I give you my answer?"

The woman smiled and nodded. Nyx threaded into the room.

———

Amanda came awake with the feeling that she was being watched. Her eyes had adjusted to the darkness and she could discern the individual shapes of furniture and decoration. But there was something in the corner of the bedroom that did not belong. Whatever it was, it nearly touched the ceiling. It was thin and hunched, its upper half arching toward Amanda.

Still intoxicated with sleep, Amanda tried to figure out what it was. Maybe it was an article of clothing hanging off the hook on the closet door.

Then it moved. A twitch.

The darkness birthed a gnarled, spidery limb. Adrenaline shot into Amanda's bloodstream. She lunged off the bed, blind to all except escape, threw open the door, without pausing to look behind her, and ran into the kitchen. She tripped over her own feet on the way to the knife block, staggered, righted herself, and pulled out four-inches of stainless steel. She stood there trembling, watching the stairs, astonished how she'd gotten here so quickly.

Something shrieked right beside her. She threw a hand over her mouth to catch the scream and wheeled around, thrusting the knife forward.

It was Nyx. She lay on the floor, legs kicking in frenzied spasms. The middle of her body was bare, stripped of fur, the skin pink and bulging as though fat slugs slithered in the space between flesh and muscle. The poor animal loosed a warbling cry. Her head shook, as boneless as a puppet, the needle teeth bared, exposing the corrugated roof of her mouth. The eyelids were pinched closed but the orbs squeezed through anyway, distorted by the pressure and flooded with burst vessels.

Amanda threaded her fingers through her hair and pulled, teeth showing in a tortured mask of terror. Was she still dreaming? What the fuck was happening?

A creak on the stairs.

Amanda glanced sharply up. Nothing. Darkness still boiled in the doorway to her bedroom, but no sign of life or movement.

Nyx screeched until blood sprayed from her throat. Amanda crouched beside her, not sure what to do with her hands. They flapped uselessly in the air. The bare skin on the side of Nyx's body twitched more violently until the ridges of deformed flesh coalesced to form the suggestion of a face. The teeth were the animal's ribs tearing bloodily through the skin, the eyes some purpled-hued organ bulging closer to the surface. Amanda screamed and slammed her fist into the face. Nyx's ribcage shattered with a dull crunch. She aspirated blood in a series of low feeble breaths, before going utterly still.

Shaking and pouring an icy sweat, Amanda raised the offending fist. It was coated in blood and a sharp fragment of rib protruded from the knuckle. When she looked down to inspect Nyx's corpse, to see if the face was still there, she abruptly found herself back in the sixties living room.

No, not exactly.

She was sitting at the foot of her bed, watching herself on the television. Onscreen, the porn actress was sitting with Amanda's television counterpart on the sixties couch, and now lifted one hand, unfolding the elbow to reveal a seam in the crook of her arm.

"Come inside," she whispered. The audio was poor, crackled with static. The woman squeezed two fingers into the seam. Skin parted from muscle with a wet peeling sound. An ozone smell wafted from the parted flesh. Amanda, sitting on the bed, could smell it emanating from the television screen.

Onscreen, Amanda stretched out her fingers—they trembled and yellow light glinted and danced off the gloss of her nails—and slid them into the fold in the woman's elbow. The woman tilted her head back, lips peeling stickily so the skin opened lengthwise from the middle, a fleshy zipper. Her teeth, evenly spaced with chinks of empty space, shone and gleamed with saliva. She closed her eyes, the lashes flirting with the crest of her cheekbone, as Amanda pushed her whole hand inside the crook of her arm.

"Be rough with me," the woman said.

Amanda seized the woman by the throat with her free hand. She leaned in, their foreheads touching, and pushed her arm deeper, up to the elbow. The woman's skin bulged obscenely. A moan escaped her lips. Amanda tightened her grip around her throat until she could feel its pulse tapping against her fingertips.

"Harder," the woman gasped.

The elbow seam flowered, the skin receding red, wet and engorged to accommodate Amanda's shoulder and head.

The Amanda sitting at the foot of her bed masturbated furiously.

Amanda's eyes burst open. She was in bed, lying with her back facing Logan's side of the mattress. Her first thought was, why am I here? With sluggish remembrance, the image of Nyx writhing on the kitchen floor sketched itself in her mind. Spurred by the recollection, she lifted her right hand in front of her face. She could feel and smell the dried blood caked between the digits. The knuckles throbbed with a dull pain. A pathetic whimper escaped her lips. In the subsequent silence, she became aware of soft respirations between the sounds of her own breathing. Someone was in bed with her. Her heart revved in panic. She held her breath for a moment—maybe it was her imagination—but the respirations continued, slow and measured. She didn't want to turn and look. Oh God, she didn't want to see. She wasn't even sure she could will her muscles into movement. If she could, she'd run back to the kitchen, but something, some remote part of her mind, told her that she would just wake up in bed again.

The mattress shifted beside her, the bedsprings creaked. Cold sweat seeped out of Amanda's pores. Her breath emerged in ragged, panicked gasps matched by the heavy, but sedate exhalations of the thing beside her. She could feel its hot breath against her neck. If she rolled over right now, she'd be staring right into its eyes. You have to run, she told herself. At least try. For Christ's sake, just try.

A tongue, warm and scaly, ran along the back of her neck.

Amanda shrieked. As if in response, the television flared into life. The woman from the stag loop was sitting on the couch staring at the camera. There was a container of antifreeze on the table and an empty bottle of prescription medication. In one hand she cupped a mound of white pills, in the other she held a stemmed wineglass filled with bright blue fluid. She palmed the pills into her mouth and knocked back the antifreeze.

Amanda rolled over. She had a glimpse of a pale form, naked with limbs horrifically distended, before it sprang on top of her, its voice the hissing static of the stag loop.

Logan returned early the next morning. The first thing he noticed was the mud on the floor, then the car battery and the axe. The battery had been nearly cloven in two, the ragged wound wet with acid. The blade of the axe also glistened with it.

Fear bubbled up inside him, raw and primal.

"Amanda," he said, bounding up the stairs, two at a time.

After a moment of agonizing silence, she answered, "In the bedroom, babe."

He stepped inside.

Amanda was seated at the foot of the bed. Her negligee was streaked with blood. She'd cut her hair into a shabby parody of a sixties bob. Her face was variously hued with the white and pink of acid burns. Her lips had been sheared off and blood streamed down her chin and neck like a garish excess of gloss. Despite her injuries, though, there was a familiarity in her appearance. It took a moment for Logan to realize what it was exactly, but when he did, his blood stilled with cold. Amanda had, through self-inflicted mutilation, performed a twisted procedure of cosmetic surgery. She'd burnt away the skin with battery acid, reducing it to malleable clay, and reshaped her facial structure so she looked like the woman from the stag loop. The resemblance, though distorted, was uncanny. Bile surged up Logan's throat. His testicles contracted in fear.

Amanda held out her hand, fingertips eaten away by acid, exposing bone.

"Come over here, baby," she said. "Let's make our own movie."

PLACENTA BRIDE

The face in the bathtub was screaming again.

Loren checked the clock on the bedside table. Three-fourteen AM. He groaned, rubbed the sleep from his eyes and slid out of bed. The hallway was impenetrably black. He moved carefully, kicking aside discarded clothes and moldering fast-food containers. Finally, his fingers encountered the smooth wooden surface of the bathroom door. He groped for the handle, gave it a turn, and stepped inside.

Even after three months, Loren still wasn't used to the smell. It emanated from the bathwater, a stink like curdled milk and dirty feet. He found the light switch and flicked it on. It took a moment for his eyes to adjust, but when they did he saw his wife's face staring up at him, framed by floating black hair.

He knelt beside the tub and dipped his hands below the surface. The water was so filthy and opaque it appeared like he'd been amputated at the wrists. He fished around, making ripples and small waves. His fingers passed over more appendages and outgrowths than he last remembered. She felt like a jellyfish. If each of its tentacles were filled with bone. And coated in hair slick with insulating oil.

She'd grown since the last time he checked on her. The screams pouring from her pale fish-belly lips must have been the result of growing pains.

Loren touched her cheek, feeling the wet gelatinous flesh beneath his fingers. Her cries tapered into a series of choked sobs. He stroked her skin until it started gluing to his fingertips then pulled away. Lifting his hand to his mouth, he sucked each digit between his lips and tasted the organic matter that clung to them. It was faintly sour, like warm yogurt. He swallowed it down, wanting to share every part of her existence.

He smiled at her and she smiled back, but something wasn't right about it. Not for the first time, Loren wondered if she was missing certain muscles in her face that would allow her to smile properly, because the thing she wore now was hard to look at: a convulsing rictus of toothless blue gums, thick drooling saliva and a tongue swollen with taste buds. Like a used extra studded condom. And behind it lurked an awareness he hadn't noticed before. Her gaze was clear and piercing, not the vacant vegetable stare he was used to. It spooked him, but he shook it off. It meant nothing. *She maintained eye contact for longer than usual, that's all*, he thought.

Loren got up, located the bottle of baby aspirin in the medicine cabinet, twisted the cap and tapped two white tablets into his palm. Filling a chipped glass with water from the tap, he returned to kneeling beside the tub.

He palmed the medicine into her mouth and lifted her head to give her a drink of water.

She drank noisily, the liquid streaming down either side of her face. A cough erupted from her chest, followed by a burp that wafted up into Loren's face, bringing tears into his eyes. He gagged, played it off as a laugh, kissed her forehead and exited the bathroom.

He wasn't going back to bed any time soon. Her presence always left him invigorated. He walked into his office and stared at the walls. The chipped and flaking plaster was adorned with pictograms rendered in black permanent marker. They told of his wife's death and resurrection, beginning with the day Loren lost everything, the end before a new beginning.

The first image in the sequence was sketched in such agonizing detail that even now Loren couldn't examine it for long without feeling a gut-churning sense of loss. It showed his wife and child dead inside the wreckage of the family car. The twisted metal rose in horned curves like the jaws of some metal monstrosity, its slaver the blood draining from the girls he'd loved more than anything else in the world—the girls who were running away, seeking a life without him.

The next illustration depicted a double funeral and was followed by six more drawings in a style unlike the rest. Their detail was minimal, the technique almost childish, but with a grim, abstract sensibility. They evoked memories Loren recalled now as he would a nightmare, one so vague yet filled with such real terror it caused him to wake in a panting, cold sweat.

One day, a couple weeks after the funeral, Loren was rooting through the freezer to fill the painful ache in his gut when he found something totally unexpected.

When his wife had given birth to their daughter, the midwife who supervised the home birth recommend she keep her placenta to provide nourishment for her body in its post-natal state. She'd taken it home, placed it in the freezer with the intention of having it grinded up into pills and quickly forgot about it. That's what Loren discovered that day while searching for something to eat, the last remaining part of his wife.

He'd taken it out and placed it on the counter. It was wrapped in plastic, the surface white with frost and freezer burn. Underneath he could discern a vaguely meaty shape, dull brown in color.

The sun had gradually melted below the horizon, elongating the shadows across the countertop until the placenta was submerged in gloom. By this time, the plastic had thawed, leaving a wide pool across the granite surface. Loren could now properly see what was wrapped inside. It was round, reddish blue and thickly veined like a raw, alien steak.

He had carefully removed it from its packing and cradled it against his chest. It smelled like old blood and the dank, fleshy musk of an exposed organ. Cold and wet, its moisture seeped through the cotton of his shirt, dampening the coils of hair on his chest. He imagined his wife's mouth pressed there, her lips glossed with saliva, and thought: *I miss you so much*. In another time, tears would have run down his cheeks, but Loren had lost the ability to shed them. Instead, his chest ached with trapped emotion, constricted and painful.

He held the placenta tighter, hoping it would ease some of the ache. The hours crawled by on amputated limbs. Darkness fell in earnest and the only sounds in the kitchen were the howling wind-hum of the refrigerator and the steady dripping of the still wet placenta.

That night, he dreamed he was standing in the kitchen. The freezer door was open a crack and belching torrents of thick, clotted blood. All around him, the walls were screaming. Then the fridge opened its…legs…and Loren was staring into his wife's sex, the labia looking more like the placenta—in color and texture—that had dwelled deep within than the silky, pink flesh he'd so often pleasured with his tongue. The slit, puffed and veiny, mewled like a newborn and he approached with the intention of soothing it into peaceful silence.

When he woke he was kneeling beside the bathtub. Water gushed from the faucet. The placenta submerged below the surface swayed to the current. Loren's position—leaning over the edge of the tub, his hands cradling the delicate thing within—brought him back to when he used to bathe his infant daughter. He remembered the way she splashed her tiny, fat arms when he lowered her into the water. The memory didn't bring tears, but the pain in his chest swelled and he vowed, with the passion and incoherence of a drunk, that he would *find* his wife again, and together they would love their child back into existence.

The bathtub ran over and Loren woke up in a shallow pool on the floor. As he staggered to his feet, he noticed the placenta's first signs of growth. It was bigger, and its veins pulsed faintly with life.

He turned the knobs, stopping the flow of water, and stared at this new development with numb interest. It felt as real as anything that'd happened since the accident. His whole life after that day had taken on the dislocated feel of a dream, like he was a loose tooth in the gums of reality. The thing in the tub was normal to him. Bending down, he caressed it with one hand and promised to be a better husband and father.

———

Now, standing before the final pictogram in the sequence, Loren smiled and pressed his palm against the image of his wife in the tub, reborn.

It was the perfect ending. Only it wasn't the end. After the placenta transformed into a copy of his wife, Loren quit his job to spend as much time with her as possible. Atoning for past sins.

For a while, he subsisted on his retirement savings. When that ran out, he was forced to consider getting another job or end up on the streets, homeless. But he couldn't leave her alone. What if she drowned in the tub? He couldn't remove her for eight hours while he was at work, either. The bathwater was her life-support, her porcelain womb. He could get a job working from home, but it would only sap more time away from his wife. He needed to find something quick and easy, which usually meant illegal. Then, one day, the answer came to him in a moment of sheer chance.

One of his coworkers had showed up unannounced. As soon as Loren cracked the door open, a look of pale ecstasy had come over the man's face. The words struggled to come out of his mouth. "What? What's inside? What are you keeping in there?"

Loren frowned at him. He didn't say a word.

"What's that smell?"

Loren flared his nostrils and took a deep breath. Nothing. His coworker pushed past him, scenting the air, running down the hallway to the bathroom.

"Don't go in there." Loren screamed. He reached the man just as he swung the bathroom door open. When his wife came into view, the man staggered back against the wall, nearly bowling Loren over. But his initial fear was quickly overcome with the same look of dumb infatuation he'd worn when the door was opened. He turned to Loren and said, "I need her right now. I'll pay you anything. Just name your price."

"Are you fucking crazy?"

The man's eyes were bulging out of their sockets, his face sheened in sweat. He looked like a rabidly horny teenage boy about to have his first sexual encounter.

"It's her smell, man. It's getting into my head. I just need her. Otherwise I'll go crazy."

Loren turned to look at his wife. She stared vacantly at the ceiling. The smell his coworker had described—could it be some kind of pheromone? He remembered watching a nature program about the mating habits of various animals and insects, and how females often used pheromones to attract a mate, or lure prey. After witnessing his wife's placenta mature into a fully developed, though malformed, human being, Loren felt anything was possible.

"Please, Loren. I need her."

Just name your price.

His mind's eye flashed on an image of his refrigerator. The door creaked open to reveal mostly empty shelves, the inside walls fossilized with stains of varying color and texture. A package of expired deli meat and a half empty bottle of mustard. Nothing more. And he was starving, had been for several days. His bank account was empty and he'd just received a letter from the power company stating that, due to unpaid bills, the electricity would be discontinued in ten days.

"How much?" Loren asked, his mouth dry.

"How much do you want?"

"Five hundred."

The man nodded, quick and decisive. He started removing his shirt. Loren seized him by the arm, stopping him just as his navel became visible.

"If you hurt her, I'll kill you," Loren said.

His coworker—Number One—nodded once again, his face twitching with aberrant desire.

Now, a knock on the door drew his attention away from the wall. He moved into the hallway and saw one of his customers—

Number Twenty-Eight—cupping his hands against the front window, trying to get a glimpse inside. They made eye contact and Twenty-Eight waved both pudgy arms over his head.

When Loren unlocked the triple deadbolts and jerked the door open, Twenty-Eight plowed into the house, his weight carrying him into the living room. Shoulders heaving, he turned to face Loren, who calmly shut and bolted the door.

"She did something to me," Twenty-Eight said.

"What are you talking about?"

Twenty-Eight rolled up the hem of his shirt, exposing a—*what the hell was it?* It looked like a growth or tumor inside his abdomen, pushing up against the sweaty, stretch-marked skin. Only it wasn't round, but instead stuck out like an accusing finger. The longer Loren stared, the more he thought of it as a sexual organ, featureless and sorely misplaced.

Could it really be a side effect of sleeping with my wife, Loren thought. He didn't notice anything similar on his own body. Perhaps a woman's placenta was constructed with the help of the father's genes, and this somehow spared him the mutation or disease or whatever else happened to Number Twenty-Eight.

"What does it feel like?" Loren asked.

"Uncomfortable in the extreme," Twenty-Eight said. "Especially when it moves."

"It moves?"

"Lower. A few centimeters every day."

"Why come to me? Shouldn't you see a doctor?"

"I thought you would know what to do. You brought your wife back. How would you not be able to explain this?"

"Should we cut it open?"

Twenty-Eight paled. "Absolutely not."

Loren shrugged, fetched a couple beers from the kitchen, handed one to Twenty-Eight and sat down in the recliner opposite the couch. Opening the tab with a hiss, he leaned back and cranked the footrest lever, crossing one leg over the other.

"Everything will be fine. We'll sit here until we figure out a solution."

Then came another knock on the door.

"Who the hell is that?" Loren lowered the footrest with a brisk, impatient movement and went to answer the door.

It was Number Seventeen, dressed in khaki shorts and socks with sandals. He grabbed Loren by the scruff of his shirt and slammed him into the wall. A frame crashed to the floor, the glass shattering with an unmistakable, sickening crack. It was a family portrait, the only one they'd taken before the accident. The knowledge struck Loren like a blow. He reached under and between Seventeen's outstretched arms, and seized him by the throat. Seventeen's eyes went wide as Loren began to squeeze, digging thumb and forefinger into the soft hollows where the carotids pumped. The grip on his shirtfront weakened and Loren shoved Seventeen into the opposite wall, smacking his head against the plaster. The man's eyes went out of focus, his face going slack and dumb.

"Are you done?" Loren said.

Seventeen replied with several short, sharp nods. Loren didn't back up just yet, though, but held his ground in front of his customer, leaving very little space between their bodies. It was then Loren noticed something hard digging into his stomach. He looked down between them. Seventeen's shirt tented outward in an obscene parody of arousal.

A scream exploded from the bathroom. The three men turned their heads at the same time. The bath water sloshed and splashed loudly, hitting the floor. Loren disengaged himself from Seventeen, meaning to run to his wife's aid, but his movement was arrested by a second scream, this one from Twenty-Eight, who fell thrashing to the floor.

His forehead was a knot of agony, the skin flushed and beaded with sweat. He struggled to push down the waist of his jeans. When they were dangling from his ankles like badly shed skin, Loren watched as the growth made its way down, retreated below the skin inches above his terrified flaccid penis, then reemerged, filling the organ like a glove so that it grew and expanded into a forceful, unnatural erection. Twenty-Eight's screams were so loud he tore the lining of his throat.

The puppet erection grew until the head ruptured, splitting

lengthwise along the urethral opening. A blur ejected itself from the widened slit and fired across the room. Loren barely dodged it before it thudded against the wall behind him.

His eyes went to the source of the blur noting its fleshy, cocoon-like structure then darted back to check on Twenty-Eight. He laid still, either unconscious or dead, blood gouting from the head of his penis, which looked more like an exploded firecracker than a sex organ.

A third scream split the air. Seventeen flailed and smashed into the door before collapsing on the entrance carpet. He didn't even have the chance to remove his shorts before his own penis exploded and an identical cocoon burst through flesh and khaki, hitting the wall with such force it bounced back and smacked Seventeen on the forehead.

The screaming from the bathtub intensified. Loren tried to make his way to his wife again, but was diverted by the cocoon hatching at his feet. The membrane bulged and tore, leaking a bluish-grey gruel that stank of chlorine and burned matches.

One brittle arm emerged, then another. The head came next, followed by a miniature naked body—a doll-sized copy of his wife, its anatomy fully developed. It regarded Loren with furtive black eyes, its movements quick, almost avian, as it began to devour its chrysalis. Loren glanced over his shoulder in time to catch the second imago crawling from its cocoon, identical in every way to the first. It too began to feast. The sounds of ripping and chewing were jarringly loud. It came to him then that the screaming from the bathroom had stopped. How long had his wife been silent? He was so enthralled by the cocoons he'd managed to tune out most of the outside world. When he looked up, he saw a dark shape filling the narrow hallway.

The silhouette was complex: a small head surmounted on angular shoulders, and myriad appendages sprouting from its lower half, some of them moving, others hanging limp. Like a living skirt. The shape took a step forward, water drooling from its body, the soles of its feet making wet, squelching sounds against the floor.

As it moved into the light, Loren recognized his wife, that

horrible parody of a smile stretching her face into ghoulish proportions. He stood still, waiting for her to approach. She extended her hand and as her long, fatly veined fingers made contact with his skin, pain exploded through his body. Ghostly fingers squeezed his throat, an invisible fist smashed his nose, and an open palm ignited fire in his cheek. This went on until he could barely stand up straight or breathe. He screamed to make it stop, but it continued unabated—then he blacked out.

He woke inside the bathtub. The water was black and warm, and thicker than normal. The twin imago stood on the edge, watching him closely. His wife crouched behind them, holding a knife at the ready. The grin was still there.

Loren reached up and touched his face. Agony bloomed under his fingertips. One eye was almost swollen shut. His teeth felt loose in their sockets.

These bruises, this pain, they're not my own—not exactly.

A flash: his wife grabbing their daughter by the arm and pulling her toward the car. Loren following close behind, begging them to stay, tears, snot and apologies gushing from his face. She screamed at him, her cheekbone blackened by a bruise, "Get the fuck away from me."

Loren's placenta wife must have seen the memory playing on his face, because she smiled even wider and gave him an encouraging nod as if to say, *do you understand now?*

He felt a burning behind his eyes, a rawness in his throat. "I was trying to fix things. Make us"—he almost said *you*, but stopped himself—"better."

All three duplicates of his wife shook their heads in unison. The original copy raised the knife, placed a silencing finger to her lips and made an incision in the hollow of Loren's throat. He flinched, blood running and mingling with the abyssal water. One of the imago leapt onto his chest, knee deep in water, and waded over to the incision. She parted the flesh with her tiny hands and crawled inside.

The procedure lasted several weeks. Flesh was excised from Loren's bones and replaced with the spare meat hanging like tumors from his wife's body. At one stage, he resembled a Victorian anatomical drawing. Striated muscle tissue exposed. Ribbons of yellow fat running through it like gilding. Then his consciousness grew permeable. Invaded by a psychic worm. The feeling was both intimately familiar and horrifically strange. His brain filled with acid and his sense of self dissolved. He floated in darkness. Anonymous and amnesiac. And from the freshly tilled soil of his being grew the seed of a new identity. It strove toward the light of awareness. Growing ever more beautiful and complex.

When it was over, Loren was no more. His old essence gathered a congregation of flies in the basement and stuck to the blades of the garbage disposal. The person in the tub who opened their eyes now was no longer a man, but a woman. The first person she saw was Loren's placenta wife.

"Hello Alyson," said the placenta wife, her words faintly guttural.

"Hello Alyson," the other replied.

MIRANDA

The following is a walkthrough for the downloadable Internet game "Miranda", alternatively known as "Photoset". The game uses the first-person shooter Build engine, and features FMV graphics for the character animations.

Before we begin, I should reiterate a few warnings that have circulated on online forums, where downloads for "Miranda" initially appeared. First, prior to gameplay, it is recommended that you take an over-the-counter pain reliever. Players have reported severe physical discomfort, acute muscle pain and headaches while engaged in gameplay. It must be stated that extended exposure to "Miranda" may lead to the development of uncontrollable muscle spasms, acute anxiety, depression, and if the player wears headphones, an unexplained disturbance of the inner ear which affects gaze stabilization. This results in darting, jittery eyes known colloquially as "The Miranda Look."

I have also have read several complaints online stating that gamepads and keyboards cease to function at certain points in the game. This is because "Miranda" requires a masturbation peripheral in order to function properly. It works best with the Japanese made "Hips" device. For those unfamiliar with this product, it resembles the disembodied torso of a woman, equipped with a pair of prosthetic breasts and lifelike genitals. It can be connected to your computer wirelessly.

As "Miranda" boots up you will notice there are no studio logos or discerning marks of creatorship. You simply find yourself alone in a darkroom. The light from an overhead lamp stains the encroaching blackness with a crimson hue. If you turn around you will see a stop bath with three black and white photographs floating on the surface. The first two are erotic close-ups of a woman's sex organ. The third shows an eyeball with the optic nerve trailing behind it. Look at each of these and then leave the darkroom through the only door. You will find yourself in the studio. The room is large and whitewashed. There is a curtained-off section in the middle. Walk toward it and part the curtain. Miranda, the model, is reclining on a sofa, a black velvet robe hugging the curves and contours of her voluptuous body. As you approach she will recommend that you find a new subject to compliment her in the next photoset. At this point you will hear a loud shrieking noise before the screen goes black. The words "DARK YGGDRASIL" appear onscreen. The words will quickly disappear and be replaced by the flashing, inverted image of a dead tree.

You will now be standing in a narrow hallway. Walk forward until you reach the first door on the left. Now, it's time for a puzzle. Knock twice using the action key. If you knock again you risk running into a game block. But if this is done correctly, you will hear an unnerving white noise reminiscent of heavy breathing filtered through static.

Continue down the hallway. The overheard fluorescents will start to flicker. Watch them carefully. The pattern of the flashes simulates the number of knocks you will need to perform on the hallway doors: two, six, three, two.

Find the next door and knock six times. A man's voice will tell you to shut up. Next door. Knock three times. The lights will go out. Now, all you have to do here is close your eyes in real life. Strange, I know, but you will not be able to advance in the game otherwise. Players who kept their eyes open during this sequence were stuck in the dark indefinitely. How the game recognizes that your eyes are closed, I cannot say. Some have suspected that the game taps into your webcam, but players without them have succeeded in solving this puzzle by shutting their eyes. Who knows?

Anyway, keep them shut until you hear the insect-like buzzing of the fluorescents. You will notice that the door is open a crack. Don't open it and whatever you do don't look inside. I realize that by saying this I'm whetting your curious appetite. Hopefully this will dissuade you: when the game first appeared on the forum of a popular gore website, a player posted a thread entitled "Door-jamb." It discussed the open hallway door and the implications of looking through the opening. The OP reported that after a few seconds of staring into the dark space between the door and its frame, he glimpsed a sign of movement, the suggestion of a pale humanoid shape skulking deeper into the shadows. As he continued to stare, he heard a loud crack as of wood splintering coming from somewhere in his apartment. He left the bedroom and entered the main living space where he realized the front door was open slightly, like the hallway door from "Miranda." The doorframe was cracked, accounting for the noise he had heard earlier. Moving to shut the door, he realized the handle was ice cold. But even more strangely, the door itself refused to move. When he looked through the opening, he realized the doorframe had *stretched*, filling the gap in the door with splintered wood and peeling scales of white paint.

Next, the OP pushed his eye against the peephole, but instead of the familiar apartment hallway with its faded, salmon carpet, he saw a vast darkness punctuated by the occasional star. There was also, he reported, two moons, one small and white and the other immense and broken, its damaged-half a ragged black wound trailing debris and particles of detritus.

Three days later, another member on the website posted a news article detailing the suicide of the OP, whose name was Michael Sloat. Allegedly, he slit his forearms from wrist to elbow. Crime scene photos appeared on the gore website shortly after. So, needless to say, I don't recommend looking through the gap in the door. Move on.

When you reach the final door knock twice. An FMV animation depicting either a man or woman will open the door. He/she might be your mother, father, sister, brother, grandmother, partner, or a composite of any of these—who cares? This person needs to die for you to proceed in the game. Again, no one knows how the game is able to create an NPC that resembles your loved ones. Nevertheless, you must now realize that the game is unique in that as you play it, it also plays you.

Some prescribe to the emergent consciousness theory, which holds that the game has developed some form of independent intelligence based on the collective cerebral input of players across the world. But this is merely conjecture. Moving on.

What we do know is that the NPC will recognize you and invite you inside. When he/she asks you questions, try not to act suspicious. Select the most innocuous answers, and most importantly lie about your job. If he/she asks if you're still wasting your time playing video games, respond in the negative. When prompted, tell him/her you need to use the washroom. Using the mouse, flush the toilet and run the tap to give the illusion that they've been used. Bring up your inventory and equip your hunting knife. Your character will draw it from the sheath inside their jacket. At this point in the game, you must have a headset connected to your computer. Call out to your loved one and they will approach the bathroom door. Swing the door open and stab him/her in the throat, effectively cutting off their screams. If you stab him/her anywhere else initially, you risk attracting the attention of the police. Then it's game over. He/she will stumble backwards. Pin him/her against the wall and open their stomach. This time the pain and shock will cause him/her to crumple down to the floor. You can get messy and yank out his/her intestines, or you can simply stab him/her through the temple or the heart, killing him/her quickly. When this is done, extract one of his/her eyes. It will appear in your inventory. You can harvest other parts of his/her body, like his/her teeth, tongue, ears, fingers, toes, nipples, penis, and clitoris, but all you need to successfully complete the game is an eyeball.

You will hear the familiar shrieking noise from earlier and the screen will once again slam to black. Back in the studio, part the curtain and have a look at Miranda. Her skin is flaking off in places, and the raw flesh underneath is striated with purple veins. Her hair is cobwebbed with delicate white filaments that quiver like living things.

You will now make use of the "Hips" device. Miranda will remove her robe, exposing herself to you. Position the masturbation peripheral so that it is lying flat, with the crotch facing you. Using the mouse, select the severed eyeball from your inventory. It will appear in your character's hand. Now, the objective is to stimulate Miranda. Many players have noted that you should begin by gently brushing your fingers along the ridge of her clavicle. Your character will alternately use his free hand and the other holding the eyeball, which he will rub against Miranda's skin, smearing it with vitreous humor. Eventually, move to her breasts, but do not stimulate the nipples right away. Massage the surrounding flesh until it is glistening with eyeball juice. Only then should you approach the nipples. Onscreen, Miranda's breathing will grow heavy. Move down her stomach, using your mouth if you wish, until you arrive at the genitals. Blowing hot air on the vulva has been shown to be effective.

Another note of caution, do not insert your penis (if you are male) in the "Hips" device. This might be common practice with other games utilizing this peripheral, but some of those who played "Miranda" have contracted a strange, and unclassifiable venereal disease. Its symptoms include a burning, silvery-white discharge, dry mouth, nausea, headaches, disorientation, and eventually, the appearance of scabs on the shaft of the penis that resemble microchips. Don't believe everything you read on the Internet, but I for one do not want to risk becoming infected with this disease.

Once you successfully stimulate Miranda, she will say: "Now, time for the offering. Show me my next subject." Insert your finger deep into her vagina. Onscreen you should see your character pushing the eyeball inside her. Use the crouch button so that you are standing level with her crotch, and are able to see the eyeball peering from the folds of her labia. Apply the button for the "print screen" command. An animation should follow in which your character produces a camera and snaps a picture of the eyeball.

POST-GAME: The game will end with real-life, handycam footage. The person holding the camera is inside an underground cave. A small headlamp vainly attempts to illuminate the massive space. Moisture drips from the walls. The cameraman's footsteps resound, loud and hollow as he approaches a tree. Like the flashing image shown earlier in the game, the tree is upside-down, growing out of the ceiling rather than the ground. Its naked, claw-like branches reach, twisted and gnarled, toward the uneven stone floor.

Out of its branches crawls a strange being. It is two meters tall and shaped like the letter Y, with a misshapen head wedged between the V. Two miniscule, rat-like eyes peer out from the pale flatness of its face. Purple veins streak its body like tiger stripes. It crawls up to the cameraman and embraces him with its stiff appendages, lacking joints, hands or fingers.

If you reached the ending of this walkthrough, you will begin to feel your skin going soft, your organs turning to liquid shit inside you. Don't worry, though, the vomiting will subside in a few days. By then you will realize, with the dehydrated, mind-expanding awareness of the mystic, that you are now a part of the collective that is Miranda—a single atom in a body spanning the limits of cyberspace.

As one of her constituents, I welcome you.

REBOUND

I broke up with my girlfriend recently. After that, it was just me and my tapeworm.

Her name was Karina.

You've probably heard the saying, "No tongue on the first date." Well, when we met at the steakhouse two weeks after the breakup, Karina went throat-deep, sliding down my tongue on an avalanche of bloody, chewed-up sirloin. In my defense, I was drunk and don't typically order rare steak, but that combined with the restaurant's poor sanitary conditions, paved the way for my dysfunctional rebound relationship.

Six months and a CT scan later, Karina had reached the length of a school bus. Imagine her running the length of my intestine. Her white, segmented body tangling and knotting like fucked up ear buds; her triangle-shaped head latching to my intestinal wall, row upon concentric row of hooked teeth clinging like R-rated Velcro that laced my shit with blood.

The doctor said she was different than most tapeworms, larger and probably not as delicate. He couldn't account for the mutation, but speculated that the hormones given to dairy cows somehow had an effect on Karina's development.

The beginning of our relationship was innocent enough. She shared my meals, from breakfast to dinner to midnight snack, and

I quickly realized which foods she preferred by the frequency of my symptoms. For instance, whenever I ate something high in glucose, like pork or pineapple, my abdominal pain would abruptly cease, reassuring me that I was being a gracious host.

Sometimes I would feel a tickle at the back of my throat, as if something was lodged there, and realized Karina was intercepting my meal, eager for her share. I knew this was impossible for your average run-of-the-mill tapeworm, and quickly chalked it up as being a result of Karina's rare and beautiful mutation. For a while I was grateful I trashed my anti-parasitic drugs.

When loneliness crept into my mind, the loud gurgling in my lower abdomen and subsequent rush of diarrhea reminded me I was never alone. I would stare into the toilet bowl and imagine Karina twisting through the tunnels of my being like a second soul.

To all those who believe they've found their soul mate, let me tell you something: some people spend their lives looking for that special someone. It becomes a relentless pursuit. What I realized is I spent too much time looking out when I should have been looking in, because my soul mate lives inside me.

Eventually, I decided to take our relationship to the next level. But conventional, human intimacy was out of the question, and a third party was necessary to help things along.

I had never done a booty call before that night, and I have to admit the idea was a little nerve-racking at first. But when Rachael stepped into my apartment and got comfortable, my anxiety subsided. We'd known each other since freshman year and there had been a lingering sexual tension ever since. When I started dating my now ex-girlfriend, Rachael went off to pursue other opportunities. But much to my surprise, she answered my text message with enthusiasm and quickly made her way over.

She sat on the couch as I slid a knife from its block and sawed off a piece of bloody steak that I'd slapped onto a cutting board. Placing it in the center of my palm, I walked into the living room and explained to Rachael the nature of my sexual fantasy. She nodded slowly with an amused smile canting the corner of her mouth.

Other than the fact that we were old friends, I chose Rachel because she was an old hand at sexual experimentation. She'd visited clubs were people drank each other's blood, known cheekily as "safe sucking." She'd also participated in suspension, and had once placed leaches on her vulva during intercourse when the skin was flushed and engorged with blood.

Standing, Rachael held out her hand, palm up, and I gave her the piece of steak, which bled through my fingers and down my forearm. Her lips parted, and the pink of her tongue emerged, with a metallic stud glistening in the light. She placed the meat on her tongue, held it there, grabbed the collar of my shirt and kissed me hard on the mouth, smearing blood on my lips and chin. When our tongues met, the piece of steak was swapped from her mouth to mine and then back again. We continued kissing, shedding clothes, when abruptly I felt a tickle at the back of my throat.

Karina had finally decided to join us.

She emerged from the depths of my throat and latched onto the piece of steak. I felt her flinch when Rachael's tongue flicked across her body, and then she tentatively returned to feast.

Meanwhile, Rachael was massaging me with one saliva-slick, blood smeared hand, and I came violently onto the cusp of her belly. *I love you Karina*, I shivered, my ears ringing from the intensity of my orgasm.

Looking back, I realize that night was one of the highlights of my relationship with Karina. But soon after, I became disillusioned with the whole affair. It seemed that every morning, when I stripped to take a shower, my body looked increasingly emaciated. Ribs and collarbone stood out in stark angularity. My skin was so pale the network of blue veins underneath resembled a roadway map of bruises. My hair was thinning, falling out and clogging the drain. Some days I was too weak to get out of bed. My asshole was fissured with small cuts from the frequency and violence of my bowel movements. It was then, staring at the reflection of the emaciated doppelgänger above the sink that I realized the damage my rebound relationship had done to my body. For days, I toiled with the idea of terminating my relationship, mulled over the various ways which I could break the news to my hidden lover.

Some days the notion brought relief, others a flood of tears that ran down my hollow cheeks. Then finally, when I was forced to call in sick because I was too weak to crawl out of bed, I slowly made my way to the kitchen, sliced a piece of steak and popped it inside my mouth.

Walking into the bathroom, I stared at the mirror, tasting copper on my tongue. Eventually, I felt that familiar tickle at the back of my throat. I had summoned her like the dark spirit she was.

I opened my mouth and saw her feasting. Slowly I lifted my hand and grabbed hold of Karina's slender, white body. She struggled, flailing between my thumb and forefinger, and I pulled with all the meager strength I had left. I could feel tightness in my guts, as if she were holding fast to the inside of my intestines. Feeling her against the back of my throat, I gagged as tears obscured my vision. Pulling harder and harder, I held her in both hands. Face flushed and gagging like a bulimic, I yanked until enough of her body emerged to tie around the faucet. Leaning back, pushing with my arms against the edge of the sink, I forced more of Karina out of my body, and the more of her that emerged I looped around the faucet. Then with one final thrust, her tail shot out, trailing a rope of saliva.

She flopped into the sink, lifeless as a Chinese noodle.

I collapsed, gulping air. With the cold linoleum floor against my cheek, I realized I was a free man again and the tears continued to flow, warm and salty against my grinning lips.

UNCONDITIONAL LOVE

She's home late again. The door slams. I hear her footsteps padding across the cold, laminate floor. A muffled curse as she trips over a textbook abandoned in the middle of the hallway. She walks toward the bedroom, perhaps to see if I'm still awake. My eyelids slam shut and I roll over so my back is facing the door. I feel her peering into the bedroom, displacing the once peaceful atmosphere, her breath heavy and reeking of her own digestive juices. The talons extruding from her fingertips make a grinding sound as they dig into the doorframe.

She stands there a moment longer, watching, doubtless making sure I'm asleep. The grinding sound is replaced by a series of clicking, choking noises, like a fistful of insects forced down someone's throat. Finally, I hear her turn and enter the bathroom. There's a pause. Then water hisses from the showerhead.

With a pang of nausea, I imagine her peeling off her clothes, heavy and soaked with a stranger's blood. The crimson bundle hits the floor with a wet slapping sound. She steps into the spray, her skin tiger-striped with red, and runs her talons through her hair to dislodge bits of gore and ragged flesh. Her lips, cracked and raw, peel back to reveal a serrated plate designed for breaking through flesh and bone. Grinning under the shower spray, she washes the plate clean of blood then spits into the drain, which swirls red with her refuse.

The shower stops with a loud *thunk*, jerking me out of my reverie, and I hold my breath in fear and anticipation. All she needs to do now is towel off then she'll be crawling into bed. But she remains in the bathroom a moment longer, and I hear a familiar sound as she wipes away the foggy dew on the mirror. She must be examining her reflection, making sure her distorted features are receding, slowly replaced by her softer, human ones.

Soon her plate will fall out, and over the next week or so— while she calls in sick at the local club where she works as a waitress—her human teeth will begin grow back. Her talons, on the other hand, she will remove during her weeklong vacation, using a pair of pliers I purchased at the department store.

Of course, the whole process will begin again in three months, when her body screams again for sustenance. Her human teeth will come loose, the gums turned soft and bleeding. She'll stand over the bathroom sink and pull them out, one by one, making room for the plate that descends from a cavity in her skull. Her talons will push up through her skin, eventually breaking through, and finally the *thing* within her will take hold.

After she storms out of the apartment in a fit of rage and hunger, I will enter the bathroom, collect her teeth from the sink, clean out the basin with a sponge and, still holding the teeth in my hands, walk over to my closet in the spare bedroom where I keep my only secret. Underneath a pile of spare blankets is a battered old shoebox. I remove the cover and gaze at what glitters inside with what can only be described as a combination of longing and nostalgia. Safely ensconced within my private box are all the human teeth she's lost over the course of our relationship. I will place the new ones inside and they'll rattle together like broken china. This is all of her I have left: hundreds of shattered pieces of her humanity.

The bathroom doors opens. Calmly now, she returns to the bedroom we shared together for the past year. Gently, she lifts the covers on her side of the bed and climbs inside. I hear the soft soughing of the sheets against her skin as she slides her feet toward me. They're cold, like ice or the grave, but I allow her to press them against the back of my legs to warm them. As long as she doesn't know I'm awake. I like to pretend that I don't know about her condition. That way a gulf of silence exists between us, a gulf that can then be filled with a mutual need. She rolls over and I can feel her breath on my face. It smells like sour meat and the peanut-stink of dead insects.

Then a whisper: "I love you."

Without opening my eyes, without saying a word, I think to myself: I love you too. With everything I am.

EARWORM

1. The Nameless Band

Damon woke in the still-dark hours of morning to find his latest one-night-stand sitting up in bed, watching him. He lived above a laundromat in a run-down area of town, and the blinking sign outside threw a neon glow through the curtains, lighting up patches of her face and body. She was naked except for her thrift-store bomber jacket, and redolent of the beer and weed they'd shared the night before. Her chemical green hair was a wild tangle about her head, and a smear of black and purple eyeliner dragged down one cheek like the warning colors of a poisonous lizard. Her smile, however, was the most unnerving thing of all. Whenever she smiled—something she'd done frequently while they'd talked at the bar—it was usually a tight-lipped curl, but the one she wore now was manic, impossibly wide, her teeth crimson with neon blood.

"I just came back from the most amazing show," she said, the words whispered through clenched teeth.

"You had a dream," Damon replied, easing back into his pillow after she'd startled him into an upright position. "Go back to sleep."

He said this more harshly than he'd intended, but he couldn't help it. She'd scared the shit out of him. His heart beat hard enough to bruise his ribcage. Adrenaline screamed through his veins, causing him to shake. He closed his eyes, doubting he would be able to sleep, but trying anyway, and then opened them again moments later to see the girl in the same position as before, that smile still curving her mouth. Neon danced with the shadows on her face, making it look less than human.

Shit. What's her name again? Damon thought. *Katrina? No. It was something unusual.* He searched his memory, wading through the booze, fear and fog. *Kira? Yeah, that's it.* They'd only met a few hours before at a local punk show. She was twenty-one, six years his junior, and one of the best lays he'd ever had. Not because she was skilled or kinky, but the opposite—they were both piss ass drunk and the sex had been a sloppy, fumbling, beautiful mess.

"I just came back from the most amazing show," she said again in that dazed, dream whisper.

"Yes we *did*," Damon said slowly, as if speaking to a child.

The headlining band was called The Blind Dead after some low-budget Spanish horror film. The bar had been packed to capacity, shoulders brushing shoulders, the atmosphere heavy with the musk of cheap weed and body odor. Once the band started, the bar's shitty sound system could barely handle the volume. The guitar sounded like a bag of cats thrown into a wood chipper, yet the crowd danced anyway. Well, maybe dance wasn't the right word. They *moved* their bodies in synch with the music, limbs loose and boneless, heads banging. The inevitable mosh pit erupted at the foot of the stage and rapidly metastasized throughout the crowd.

Before he knew it, Damon had been absorbed by the collective, becoming a single cell in a much bigger organism. He rubbed against friends and strangers, their heat absorbed into the fabric of his clothing, his skin. Closing his eyes, the world spun and twisted like he was the center of a galaxy gone haywire. When his eyelids peeled open, he saw Kira, her head lolling to the music, face shining with sweat that reflected the bar's scanty light. She smelled unwashed, earthy and primal. His senses nearly short-circuited. His nostrils brimmed with her scent. His eardrums throbbed with the band's gunfire drumming. And soon his mouth was filled with the taste of Kira's tongue as she stumbled toward him and placed an unexpected kiss on his lips. All in all it was a pretty good—

"Not that show," Kira said, bringing Damon back to the neon-tinted darkness.

He shook the memories of that evening from his mind and realized he was having trouble reconciling the Kira from the bar with the one looking down at him now, grinning feverishly and bathed in crimson light. It was like he'd gone to bed with one woman and woken up with another. *Only this one isn't exactly a woman, is she now, Damon? Shut the fuck up,* he told the nagging Vincent Price voice in his head. Damon hated anything even remotely scary. He still watched horror films through the spaces between his fingers.

Whenever he was alone that voice—the one that sounded oddly like Vincent Price—would bubble up from his subconscious and fill him with suggestions of what might be lurking in the corners where the shadows were darkest. *Perhaps a blood-crazed murderer found his way into your apartment while you were at work,* or, *this building is old, who knows how many spirits call it their home.* The voice was having a field day now, composing an entire *Thriller-* style rhapsody about Kira's odd behavior. Damon did his best to ignore it. The voice of rationality strove to overpower the fear. *Obviously, Kira is a sleep walker,* it said, informed by a wrinkled life-style magazine Damon had flipped through once while waiting at the doctor's office.

Otherwise known as somnambulism, he now remembered—a word he associated with coffins and shambling white-faced weir-does—*the person afflicted appeared to be sleeping with their eyes open, while their minds were still submerged in the mire of dreams.* They were basically puppets to their own subconscious. The thought didn't reassure him. It had the opposite effect, sending a fresh chill down his back. He decided to steer his mind in a different direction. At this rate, he was careening toward full-bodied panic.

"What show?" he asked, thinking it was better to focus on the little details than the bigger picture, with its horror movie implications.

Kira's jaw unlocked and her lips began forming words normally. It was like watching her come awake from paralyzing sleep. Only Damon wasn't convinced she was actually awake. That dream puppeteer was still tilting his control bar in some far-off place, guiding her strings with a deft hand.

"They didn't have a name," she said. "I don't remember them playing any instruments either, but I heard them."

Damon frowned. To humor her, he asked, "What venue?"

"It was a basement show. I've never been there before."

For some reason, this vague response triggered a mental image so vivid Damon thought he'd been transported to the basement in question. It was low ceilinged, musty with dust and the smell of damp. The walls were patterned with oblong patches of paint a shade darker than the rest, as though band posters had once adorned them but had long since been removed. When the image blinked out of existence, Damon experienced a brief spell of vertigo.

When he recovered, he said, "What kind of music was it?"

"Punk. Their sound was raw and violent. I could feel it in my blood like contact dye."

And that's enough for me, Damon thought. He was too tired and overwrought to listen to this bullshit any longer. To make matters worse, a headache rapped on his skull, demanding entry. He wanted to sleep and for that to happen, he needed Kira to snap out of it.

Impatience crept into his voice. "What the hell are you talking about? Go to sleep, you're freaking me out."

Kira didn't go back to sleep. She stood up, swaying on the lumpy mattress, and started dancing to a beat she heard only in her head. Her feet were bare, filthy, the polish chipped. Damon couldn't remember if she'd been wearing shoes on their walk home, or if she'd taken them off before entering the apartment. He was about to ask her when another scenario entered his mind. What if she'd actually snuck out in the middle of the night, shit-faced and disoriented, to an after-hours basement show? Damon had drunk enough beer and done enough drugs to tranquilize him into a skid-coma, so it wasn't impossible that she slipped away without his notice.

Bleary-eyed, he peered across the room at the alarm clock. It was four twenty-seven. When did they get home? Two-thirty? Did that give her enough time to hit another show and make it back in time to scare the shit out of him? He guessed so, assuming the clock was right. It had a habit of slowing down or speeding up on its own, so he couldn't be sure. Then again, how did she manage to get back into the apartment without a key? Did she pocket his only set before leaving?

Instead of asking her outright, he said, "Kira, are you fucking with me?"

She said nothing for several seconds. Then her impossible smile returned, stretching her face beyond recognition. Damon's bowels turned to water.

2. An Orgy of Infrasound

A finger jabbed him in the ribs. Damon jumped, startled, and looked up to see his best friend, Cid, pounding back a beer. He was no longer in his apartment. That much was obvious. The light was different, so was the musty, dirty sock smell.

They were sitting across from each other at a small, circular table. The window at Cid's back framed a night scene of street lamps and wet glistening asphalt. A pinball machine chimed and flashed in the corner. They were inside a bar, the same bar where Damon had seen The Blind Dead with Kira. Was that yesterday, or the night before? He couldn't remember. It felt like only seconds ago he'd been watching Kira's face twist into that unnatural grin. *Am I losing my fucking mind*, he thought with a stab of anxiety.

"*Hey, man. You all plugged in up there?*" Cid said tilting his head to one side like a confused lapdog. It sounded like he was speaking underwater.

Damon blinked a few times, trying to hit the reboot button on his brain. When Cid spoke again, his words sounded clear and Damon was relieved.

"You alright bud?" Cid said.

"Yeah, yeah, I'm fine. I just sort of zoned out, I guess."

"What's the last thing you remember me saying?"

Damon's silence was answer enough. He didn't remember a fucking thing. It was awkward and more than a little troubling, but there was no point hiding the fact. He shrugged his shoulders and scrunched up his face by way of apology.

Cid laughed. "Jesus. Are you high?"

"No." Damon shook his head. "I don't know. Just confused and tired. I didn't get much sleep last night." But he wasn't convinced that was the truth. He wasn't convinced of anything.

A distorted guitar riff tore through his head, blotting out the world. He saw Kira, her too-wide smile and the silhouette of concert performers he somehow identified as the nameless band she'd mentioned. The sudden onslaught of images made him flinch. Were these fragments of a memory or a dream? If he thought too hard about it, a sharp pain started at the base of his skull. Maybe he *was* high, had been dosed with something— roofies, acid, or a new grifted pharmaceutical that worked its way into the scene. What else could explain his disorientation?

"All good, man," Cid said and grinned sideways. He gestured to the full glass of beer in front of Damon. "Have a drink. Relax. You didn't miss much. I was just ranting about my usual paranoid bullshit."

Damon lifted the glass to his lips, a patient taking his medicine. The taste was familiar and comforting. The world started to make sense again.

He looked at Cid like he was seeing him for the first time. He was dressed in his usual uniform: faded boot cut Levi's, nonde-script black t-shirt, and black jean jacket adorned with pins and patches of his favorite punk and metal bands and allusions to obscure cult horror films. His hair was self-cut and unkempt and he smelled like cigarettes and an undercurrent of—what was it? Rotten meat? No, that couldn't be right. Damon sucked in another breath through his nose. The smell, whatever it had been, was gone. All that remained was the spectral trace of stale cigarette smoke.

"Ever hear of MKUltra?" Cid asked.

Damon shook his head. Over Cid's shoulder, he could see the street, deserted and dark. The sky didn't look right, but Damon couldn't put his finger on why. Before he could get to the root of his observation, Cid's voice reeled him back in.

"It was the code name for a bunch of secret research projects led by the government in the fifties and sixties. Mind control shit. Most of the test subjects didn't even know they were part of an experiment. They were involuntarily dosed with LSD, hypnotized and tortured—all kinds of fucked up shit." Cid was getting more and more agitated with every word. Now that he was finished, though, his demeanor had relaxed and he stared absently around the room. Then, finally, he faced Damon again and said, in the calmest tone imaginable, "It's all declassified now. You can read some of the original documents online."

Damon fought hard to suppress the bubbles of anxiety rising up within him. It was like Cid had been reading his thoughts, tuning into his paranoia. *What if I told you, Damon, that you were a test subject in an underground experiment,* said the Vincent Price voice. *Why else would you remember this conversation? Yes, I said remember. You aren't experiencing this interaction in real time. You're remembering it.* Price let out his trademark cackle, rising waves of sinister laughter pounding through Damon's skull. He shoved the imaginary voice aside like he would a drunken asshole bumping into him at the bar.

"Sure," he said to Cid. "What are you getting at?"

Cid spread his hands as if to say, "Hold on a sec, I'm trying to get to the point here." He took another pull of his beer, careful to replace the bottle in the ring of condensation it formed on the table when he was finished, and resumed what was shaping up to be one of his many, wild conspiracy theories. Damon knew what he was going to say before the words came out of his mouth.

"I don't think these mind control experiments ever stopped," Cid said, leaning forward, his chest pressed against the table's edge.

"What do you mean?"

"I've been picking up on these signals. The air around us is a total orgy of infrasound."

A frown creased Damon's forehead.

Cid stuttered out an explanation, "Infrasound is an extremely low frequency sound, way below the limit of human hearing. It's everywhere. You're picking up on it now without even being aware of it, but I managed to train myself to tune in and hear specific voices stealthily designed to target the subconscious mind."

This statement did little to ease Damon's anxiety, conspiracy bullshit or no. He wasn't right in the head, and anything Cid could have told him would have driven another nail of paranoia into his already quivering brain. And the Vincent Price voice only got louder as the conversation continued: *Is this reality? Or is it a dream? In this sleep of death, what dreams may come? Ha-ha-ha-ha-ha-ha!*

Goddamnit, shut the fuck up, Damon thought desperately.

Another guitar riff drowned out his senses, followed by a second flash of the nameless band in silhouette. A lead singer, bassist, guitarist and drummer, all of them physically distorted like they were originally one vast shape struggling to remain separated. They kept phasing into one another, their outlines trembling and blurring. Damon blinked hard.

When the hallucinations subsided, he tuned briefly back into reality, catching only snippets of Cid's monologue, "...project 68... using cues to trigger...almost hypnotic alpha wave state... controlled doses of alcohol and marijuana."

He shook his head to clear it. Nausea bloomed in his stomach like a poisonous flower. He had a sudden, vivid image of himself puking blood on the table. The thick, red fluid filled his glass. It overflowed, pouring from the edges of the table in noisy streams, spattering the floor and his shoes. Cid's face was flecked with gore, but he still rambled, on and on and on and on.

Another riff, and this time Damon thought he could hear other instruments under the steady thrumming, whine of the guitar. Punk music. The sound was raw and primal. It was the only way he knew how to describe it, using the same words Kira had whispered to him that night. When was that? Yesterday, last month, last year? Had it even happened?

The music rose in pitch. Crunchy guitar chords ripped through his head, cymbals crashed against his eardrums, and a voice that couldn't possibly be human wailed into a voice amplifier: *You're all fucking filth*, it sang, *You all deserve to die / Cut yourselves open / Take everything out / Put it on the table.*

A loud pop and Damon was back. Cid rambled on as if nothing had happened, "They're targeting counterculture movements, minorities," he was saying. "Queers, immigrants, hippies with an allergy to bathing, you name it."

The lyrics still echoed in Damon's mind as he said, "Counterculture movements? What are you talking about? Who's targeting them?"

"You drifting off again, man? It's the government. All those old pissed off white dudes who can't roll with the times. They've developed sonic weapons and they've found a way to sneak them into our music. The punk scene is an easy target with its fury and anarchic sentiment. I think they're going to wipe us out first."

"This sounds fucking insane. Even for you, Cid," Damon said. The lyrics had faded into silence, leaving him with a deep feeling of unease. "What do the weapons do? How do they get them into our music?"

"I'm not exactly sure, but maybe the musicians are already infected and unwittingly emit some kind of infrasound frequency."

"Infected?"

"Yeah, the weapons cause tumors to develop in the ear canals, tumors that'll gain sentience and worm their way into the brain, ultimately controlling the host like a puppet. Soon they'll blast signals"—Cid jabbed a finger in the air like he was firing a laser beam from under his fingernail—"into the decision-making part of the brain, compelling the host to surgically remove parts of their body until they're an empty sack of skin controlled by the earworms."

The lyrics repeated in Damon's memory: *You're all fucking filth / You all deserve to die / Cut yourselves open / Take everything out / Put it on the table.* What was going on? Was this some kind of sick joke? Everything Cid described matched perfectly with what was happening to him. *Holy fuck*, he thought, *I am losing my mind.*

"The act of removing one's body parts, in this case, is called a Transhuman Panotomy. Get it? Transcending humanity by removing everything that makes you human. That's the delusion. You're going to remove everything and die. You're not going to transcend to some loftier state of existence like the earworms are promising you, *you're going to fucking die.*"

"Is the nameless band one of these sonic weapons?" The words dribbled out of Damon's mouth like an involuntary gush of vomit.

"You know about that?" Cid said, his shock palpable.

I just came back from the most amazing show.

"What can you tell me about them?"

"Not much," Cid admitted. "They're part of all this, though. Ground zero. Something horrible in the shape of a band that speaks in punk music tones. They're dangerous, man. I don't think any of us can really understand what they're all about."

Damon was listening, but staring outside the window over Cid's shoulder. He finally realized what was wrong with the sky. It was fake, a matte background on a cheap movie set. He wasn't inside a bar. This wasn't reality, or a memory—it was hell.

"Why?" Cid said. "Do you know someone who's seen them?"

3. Transhuman Panotomy

"You fell asleep on me."

Damon reluctantly opened his eyes and saw Kira perched over him, her face a shadow one minute and a mask of red light the next. She still wore the same predatory smile. A whimper rose in

Damon's throat, threatening to break free. He tried to swallow it down, but it lodged there like a stone. Kira cupped his cheek and stroked the hair on his temple with her fingertips, humming some tune, a very familiar tune.

"You were having a bad dream," Kira cooed.

Damon threw her off him and she hit the wall with a soft thump. He skidded up to his feet and ran, stumbling, toward the bathroom. Slamming and locking the door behind him, he turned and stared at his reflection in the mirror.

"Okay," he breathed. "You're awake." He punched his forehead hard enough for his vision to blur momentarily. "You're real. Flesh and blood."

Using his thumb and forefinger, he peeled back his eyelid and examined the pupil for any sign of drug reaction. It shrank in the light. But that didn't necessarily rule out the possibility of drugs. Maybe if he forced himself to vomit, it would clean out his system. Like that one time, during a bad mushroom trip, when he noticed —movement from the edge of his vision.

Looking down, he saw a black and segmented thing slither down the drain. Its body was mottled with blind milky eyes—or were they mouths?—that seemed to possess a dull sort of intelligence. Woozy dread trickled along Damon's nerves. Then he screamed until he tasted blood in his throat as a supernova ignited in his skull. The agony was brief but apocalyptic, the worst headache imaginable. When he looked in the mirror again, his left ear was gushing blood. A dark red stream painted a swath down his jawline, neck and shoulders.

Outside the door, muffled but unmistakable, came the whispered tones of Kira's voice, "They're making babies inside your brain," she said. "Little souvenirs from the nameless band." She started to giggle. Her feet beat against the floor in rhythmic cadence. She was dancing.

Damon gripped the sides of his head with shaking hands, not wanting to believe what she had told him. Somewhere music started to play. Savage drumbeats gave way to dirty guitar chords and lyrics: *You're all fucking filth / You deserve to die / Cut yourselves open / Take everything out / Put it on the table.*

It was coming from inside the walls. Damon clamped his hands over his ears, one palm sliding against the steady rush of blood. Under the music, he heard a gnawing sound from inside his own skull, like cereal crackling in freshly poured milk, and knew by way of instinct it was the tumors, the earworms, feasting on his brain tissue.

A knock on the door. "Let me in, Damon. Let's dance."

"Fuck off," he screamed.

"Fine. I'll start without you." A pause that seemed to last forever. "You keep the knives in the first drawer, right?"

Damon slammed the door with an open palm, leaving a bloody handprint. "Don't even think about it, don't you fucking dare."

The music heightened in volume until Damon's teeth vibrated and a wave of dizziness washed over him. He had no other choice. He couldn't allow Kira to slice her body open. He clutched the door handle, hesitated.

"Fuck me."

He twisted the knob and the door opened, but the apartment outside was no longer familiar. The floors were raw cement, the walls painted an unsightly brown, like liquid shit. A single tube of fluorescent light—the others were dead husks—illuminated the space. The air smelled like a slaughterhouse.

"Kira," he screamed, but his voice was drowned out by the music, louder now that the door was open. It was coming from somewhere down the hallway.

He took a step onto the cement floor, cold under his bare feet, and shivered. For the first time tonight he realized he was completely naked. A bolt of panic surged through him. Cupping his dick and balls with bloody hands, he cautiously made his way down the hallway, toward the music. At about what seemed like halfway, he noticed he was singing along with the band, pausing between each line to utter a hoarse explosion of laughter.

At the end of the hallway, he rounded a corner and found himself in a familiar room. The atmosphere was musty and the ghosts of band posters haunted the walls. It was the basement where Kira had seen the nameless band. And speaking of Kira, she was standing next to an old wooden table, the room's only piece of furniture, a blood-caked knife gripped in one hand. A jagged incision ran from below her breasts down to where her pubic hair started. Her intestines spooled out on the floor, steaming in the cold air.

Kira smiled at him, her mouth awash in red, and raised the knife in greeting. A black worm squeezed out of her ear and slapped wetly on the floor.

"Let's transcend together," she said, but it didn't sound like Kira. The voice was oddly musical and crackly like an old record.

Kira took a step toward him, her bare foot nudging a coil of intestines across the gritty cement. She reached into the incision and pulled out something that may have been her liver, lifted it to her nose, inhaled its muggy, fleshy aroma, and took a bite. It looked tough, resisting the pressure of her jaws, blood and clear fluid squirting out on her face and forearm. After some effort, she managed to tear off a piece and started to chew, her eyes rolled to whites.

Damon didn't even scream. The shock was so deep he could only turn and walk briskly in the direction he'd come. His head was down and not three steps away he bumped into another person. He looked up and stared into the ravaged face of his best friend. Cid smiled, exposing a mouth void of teeth and tongue. Even some of the gums had been scraped away like the guts from inside a pumpkin. Damon spared a glance down. Cid's stomach was slashed wide open, the edges of the incision curling outwards. The cavity was empty and the ridges of his spinal column were visible at the back. Damon's eyes returned to Cid's face and started to film with tears as worms wriggled in profusion from Cid's eye sockets, pushing the orbs outward until they popped free and dangled against his cheeks from their optical nerves. In their place, the worms balled up and formed ersatz eyes that gleamed blackly in the dim light.

Cid proffered his knife and Damon accepted it in a trembling hand. He was still singing along to the music. Cid's lips were moving too, but no sound emerged. To a combined chorus of the nameless band and the worms gnawing away at his brain, Damon pressed the knife into the soft tissue of his abdomen.

PISS SLAVE

The guy on the missing person poster is your typical college jock. He's popular with his fraternity and enjoys all the wild parties, drinking, and sex that come with the territory. He has a closet full of name brand clothes, a new car and trophy girlfriend to ride shotgun. He's tall, gym-sculpted. His square jaw is dappled with golden stubble, his hair thick and wavy—all in all a pretty good-looking dude. But that was more than a year ago, before knuckles and kneecaps destroyed his face. Before he became my latrine and punching bag.

Now he's folded into himself like a dying spider. His face has lost its roundness, and his hair's been shaved down to the scalp. His skin is so completely covered with bruises and lacerations that it doesn't look like skin anymore, more like a swathe of badly cured leather. One eye is swollen to the size of a fist, the lid and area around it black with coagulated blood.

He smiles up at me, a bloody froth bubbling through the spaces left by missing teeth, his gums rotted and glistening under the naked bulb on the ceiling. His undamaged eye finds mine and without thinking I drive my fist into his temple. He's so fragile it's like hitting a child. He takes the blow like a loving touch.

Opening my hand, I slap the crown of his head, hard, the smack resounding hollowly off the wet concrete stairs behind us.

Where I'm standing isn't so much a room as an alcove: six feet long by three feet wide. A steel door on the far wall is chained and bolted. Between the door and stairs is a piss soaked sleeping bag, two doggy dishes: one with a scrim of dirty water and the other filled with raw hamburger. A rusted bucket overflowing with watery shit leans dangerously close to the foot of the sleeping bag. And to top it off, the walls are graffitied with the kid's blood, sprays of all thicknesses and designs, the filigree of a mad painter's brush.

Like those who came before me, I'd come to contribute my own art.

Bruises slowly form along the ridge of my knuckles—tattoos of violence—and I flex them until they pop. The kid makes a noise halfway between a whimper and a laugh. I punch him again, this time squarely in the nose. Blood splashes over my fist and forearm. It's not even red like blood should be, but a diseased blackish brown; the way horror movie blood looks under a grimy filter. I go down on one knee, smile briefly into his face, and hit him with an uppercut. His leftover teeth clack together like shards of ceramic. He gurgles blood and flattens on the sleeping bag, which squelches under his weight.

Straddling the kid, I rain blows on his face, knocking it from side to side, each rotation throwing up a phlegmy string of blood. Then something in his neck pops and I stop. The kid goes limp. I check for a pulse. Faint but still there. Thank fucking Christ. The Raggedy Man, purveyor of all things immoral, was very specific about not killing the merchandise. I can do whatever I want to his so-called piss slave as long as I didn't snuff him. Some people shit in his mouth and force him to swallow it. Others stab him in nonlethal areas with switchblades and screwdrivers. Some crazy fucker even cut off his ears, forcing the Raggedy Man to stitch them back on. If you look closely enough, you can see the poor job he did sewing everything back together.

I didn't plan on shitting in the kid's mouth or cutting off his ears, though. I paid three hundred dollars in crisp ATM twenties to beat the living shit out of him and that's what I was going to do.

The thing is, I have a near-crippling case of internalized

aggression and no safe way of releasing it. It's been a bad year. My family ripped apart, leading to sleepless nights and days spent in a fog. I dealt with it the only way I knew how, with a steady dose of alcohol and barbiturates. The drugs kept me from dreaming, but my waking life had become a nightmare I couldn't wake from, and getting fucked up wouldn't help for much longer. I needed something else. I needed a proper outlet.

In theory I could have beaten the shit out of my boss for being such a prick, or kicked my dad in the balls for neglecting me as a kid and cheating on my mom, but none of these were the answer. This is where the piss slave came in. He was a one of a kind commodity that allowed the user to release aggressions without fear of repercussion. The piss slave was a kid who was systematically abused to the point of enjoying it. He especially liked it when someone showered him in urine, a fetish that earned him his street name.

He isn't just one person, the Raggedy Man had said to me as he folded the bills and stuffed them into his jacket pocket, *He's you, he's me, he's everyone. A mirror, a cipher. He isn't human anymore.*

Do I care that this kid used to be someone's son, someone's boyfriend, or at the very least, a human being that mattered? No. He's a tool, a means to an end, and I intend on making my money count.

I wrap my hands around his throat and lift the piss slave into a sitting position. He's laughing again, a demented giggle that raises hackles on the back of my neck.

I kiss him passionately with my knuckles. His giggle stutters like a song on a bad Internet connection, but doesn't stop. It's getting on my nerves so I make a point of hitting him in the mouth and, quickly after that, in the throat. His upper lip splits along the cleft, leaving a wide open-curtain gash up to his nose, spilling blood on the broken enamel of his teeth and over his chin. He's still giggling, a wheezing he-he-he-he through his now constricted larynx.

I put my hand under his chin and lift his head to face me. Peeling open one of his eyelids with my thumb, I spit in his eye. The orb jitters in its socket, the whites cracked with fissures of bright red. I double-punch him on the corner of the forehead, where the skull is thick. He makes a warbling cry that's almost avian, and lets his head roll back along his shoulders, leaving his throat exposed. I stare. A vein pulses in his neck, and I remember…

Mom in a hospital bed. Veiny hands resting on starched white sheets. A taped IV on one wrist and a plastic identification bracelet. Sunlight fracturing off the bald curvature of her skull. And that vein, quivering like something left out in the cold. Alive but just barely. Dad drove the final nail home when he fucked one of his clients and left with an overstuffed duffle bag. I held her hand as the last breath rattled out of her lungs. She died with her eyes open, staring at me. In that look, I saw everything, or at least I thought I did. The fragility of it all. The razor wire tightrope walk we perform everyday. And for what? To die with our eyes open, heartbroken and stinking of urine?

It takes everything for me not to scream. I'd cry if I could, but I haven't done that in over eight years, not even at Mom's funeral. I'm afraid something's wrong with me. I want to cry, more than anything, but the anger's heated my tears to vapor.

The memory sobers me. I'm abruptly aware of the pain in my knuckles, a steady throb like the pulse of that neck vein. My chest is full of broken glass, my breathing heavy and ragged. Nausea slithers up my throat but I manage to swallow it down.

Driven by a need to understand, I genuflect in front of the piss slave and right him into a similar position. We stare at each other, level now, even though his eyes—flooded with burst vessels—have a tendency to wander. Holding his shoulders, my hands slippery with sweat and blood, I ask, "Why don't you leave this place? Go back home?"

He remains silent, his eyes darting, his head lolling like a child unable to stay awake.

"Why are you letting me do this to you?"

Still nothing.

"Are you afraid the Raggedy Man will kill you if you try to leave?"

The piss slave titters.

"Answer me, you fuck." I raise a hand to slap him but it hangs in the air, frozen.

The titter mutates into a cackle. My open palm arches toward his cheek, a loud clap of flesh on flesh. He flinches, but the laughter persists. I slap him over and over again.

"Fight back, you fucking coward."

The laughter rings in my ears, growing louder by the second. Anger boils up inside me again. I stand up, unzip my fly, and direct a stream of steaming yellow piss into the kid's mouth. He splutters, chokes, and falls silent as a look of ecstasy spreads across his face. I don't even know why I'm doing this, but it feels inevitable, necessary.

As the stream begins to thin and finally taper off, whiteness creeps into the corners of my vision. Was I going to pass out? I look down at the piss slave. Holes are opening on his chest and shoulders, circular mouths dilating and shrinking as they drink the final dregs of urine trickling over the kid's body. The skin inside each hole is smooth, pink and coated in pearlescent mucus.

I blink, horrified, as the whiteness invades my vision. Something warm and wet douses my face. When I open my eyes—when did I close them? —I'm looking up at a fat, uncircumcised dick spitting urine into my face. Every nerve in my body is ignited with unbelievable, all-consuming pain. The feeling is almost transcendental. I lift my trembling chin toward the stream like it's a blessing of rain in a drought. The confusion of switching bodies is only temporary. Within seconds I completely forget the anger that drove him to desecrate me with fists and urine. I know only pain. It's all I have and it's beautiful.

Pain is the great unifier. The man in the suit knows this on some primitive level. It's why he came to me. He funnels his pain into me for my pleasure, and his guilt is transformed into pain. It's the only cycle that matters. Suffering unites us all. Everyone has experienced pain and we connect with others through this common bond. No race, religion, or gender can escape the beautiful reality of pain. This is why, above all else, that I am a teacher.

He's empty now and quickly stuffs himself back into his pants, ashamed. Give me more. Please. I'm thirsty, so thirsty. The other mouths swallow the remaining drops and seal shut with a wet sucking sound.

A denim-clad knee strikes me in the face. The alcove spins in on itself, a blur of blood and concrete, and I hit the sleeping bag, laughing. I can't help it. I have nothing to say anymore. Laughter is all I have. It's the only expression that makes sense.

Sometimes when I'm in bed alone, high on the painkillers the Raggedy Man gives me to help me sleep, I remember my old face. Women touched that face, kissed it, pressed their cunts against it. I vaguely recall the smell, a rich musk of moist flesh and dark places. I remember my parents, or at least I think I do, and another woman whose smell I don't know—my older sister. She has two kids, or at least I think she does.

The guy punches me in the gut. A thin spume of vomit ejects from my mouth, adding yet another color to my sleeping bag.

"Why are you letting me do this to you?" the man asks. He's breathing hard.

The guilt always sets in once they've emptied themselves on me.

"What's wrong with you?"

I laugh again, the only suitable response.

"What happens if I get you out of here?"

I've heard this before and will hear it again.

"Will that guy, the Raggedy Man, try to kill us?"

More laughter.

I close my eyes against the world. An arm reaches under my back and I'm lifted off the sleeping bag.

"Don't make a fucking sound," the guy says.

My laughter continues. A hand clamps over my mouth. We emerge into the rain slick street. I know by the smell. It's fresh, not the stale perfume of my blood and waste. A car door opens. The guy throws me into the back seat. I hear him get behind the wheel and start the engine.

When my eyelids peel open, I'm looking out a windshield dappled with rain. I engage the wipers and see the street clearly, neon reflected on puddled asphalt, and the grey night of a chemically poisoned sky. The kid is still laughing in the backseat. He stinks so bad my nostrils burn.

The Raggedy Man is nowhere in sight. I shift into drive and navigate through a maze of seedy backstreets until I reach a familiar stretch of road. Flicking the turn signal, I take a ramp onto the highway and drive into the night. My eyes dart to the rearview mirror. The kid is balled up with laughter.

"I'm doing this for your own good. I don't have a choice. This is no way to live."

My mother's image flashes in my mind's eye. The anger is mostly gone now, but my veins are singing with adrenaline.

It takes fifteen minutes to reach the rock quarry. I park the car, lift the kid into my arms and carry him several yards through the dark and rubble. When I reach a spot far from potential witnesses, I throw the kid onto the ground. His laughter falters only for a moment as he makes contact with the uneven, rock-strewn earth. Then it resumes in earnest, echoing off the towering mounds of stony debris around us.

I shake my head at the kid. "You're not human anymore. The Raggedy Man was right." Squatting, I lift a heavy stone off the ground. "And that's no way to live."

I close my eyes and raise the stone in both hands above my head.

Opening them, I look up at the guy in the shabby suit and tie, hefting a rock over his head like some holy idol. As he brings it down on my skull, I smile. And for the first time in over eight years I begin to cry.

AN INTERVIEW

"Okay, I made it," Jeremy said into the wireless headset hooked over his ear.

Climbing out of his shitbox car, he closed the door and started up the path. Gravel crunched like small bones underfoot. The house at the end of the driveway was completely unlit, a deeper darkness against the night sky. Its angles were outlines sketched in moonlight, like something an artist began drafting but quickly abandoned.

His headset crackled, making him jump.

"You still have a signal. I'm impressed," came the voice of Laney Clarke, his editor and sometime fuck buddy. "That's not how these things usually work."

Jeremy laughed nervously. "Don't date yourself. You can probably get a signal on the moon, nowadays. And besides, I'm still in the city."

"But you're also on Ladysman395's property," she said in a spooky, wavering voice. "Who knows what kind of booby traps he has rigged around the place."

"That's exactly what I want to hear before interviewing this psycho."

Sometimes Jeremy wondered why he worked for Laney's stupid underground e-zine—then he remembered the way her skin looked under his hands, its soft curves adorned with gothic tattoos. *You weak, testicle-brained fuck*, he thought.

"Relax, I'm playing," she said. "Do you actually think I'd send you into a trap? The guy only kills women. That's why I sent you. I've been feeding his ego for weeks on an Onion chatroom, posing as a male admirer. He's about to get publicity. It would be—" she paused, groping for the right word "—counterintuitive for him to kill you."

"Whatever you say." Jeremy climbed the front steps. The old wood creaked under his soles. A frown creased his forehead as a disturbing thought occurred to him. "You know how no one's found the bodies? What if the dude has them arranged around the kitchen table, like some fucked up dinner party?"

"There isn't enough left of his victims to sit at a table. Didn't you look at the pictures he posted online?"

"Fuck no. I thought it would be better if I didn't see anything. That way it would be easier to pretend the guy doesn't kidnap women and turn them into prime cuts."

She sighed, a typical, extravagant Laney sigh. "You're supposed to be an admirer, you dumbass. You should have looked at the pictures. He's probably going to want to talk about his work."

"His work," he said. "You're acting like he makes coffee tables for a living."

"You know he can probably hear you, right?"

Jeremy leaned back and peered up at the dirty windows. "I doubt he's even home. There isn't a single light on in the house. Do I just knock?"

"Yeah, go for it," Laney said. "I'll hang up when he answers the door. Do you remember the interview script?"

"Yeah, yeah," he raised his fist to the door. Paint was peeling off in curls like wood shavings. His mouth went dry. "Ah fuck me."

Jeremy knocked, twice. The sound was ominously loud. He waited in silence. Didn't realize he was holding his breath until he sucked in a loud mouthful of air. A minute passed. Two. No answer. He listened for the sound of footfalls, heard nothing.

Laney's voice made him jump again, "You good?"

"Jesus. Yeah, I'm fine. There's no answer."

"Try the door."

"What?"

"He said he might be in his study. He probably didn't hear you."

"Are you kidding me?"

"Trust me. Things will be a lot worse if we walk away."

"What the hell does that mean? Worse how?"

"Just go inside. It'll be fine."

"Famous last words." The laughter that trembled out of his chest carried a hysterical edge.

"Get your shit together and go inside."

The tone of her voice sobered him faster than a bucket of ice water. His hand trembled as he reached for the doorknob and gave it a twist. The door creaked open. As soon as he was inside, multiple hands reached out of the adjacent wall to grab him. He flinched, but quickly realized the dark was only playing tricks on his mind. They weren't hands, limp and decayed in death, but hanging tongues of wallpaper. Jeremy sucked in a lungful of air. It smelled strongly of metal. No doubt about it, the place was definitely abandoned.

"Laney, something's not right. I need to get out of here."

Jeremy turned and reached for the doorknob, but it was no longer there. He wasn't standing in the same place he was five seconds ago. In front of him was a long hallway terminating in a steel door.

The words that came out of his mouth sounded like a cross between a whimper and a scream.

"The door's gone. The whole place just changed."

"What do you mean changed? It's dark, I'm sure you just—"

"The door *disappeared*."

"Like in the cartoons? Did someone build a brick wall behind you while you weren't looking?"

"There's something seriously wrong here. Call the police."

"We can't get the cops involved, you know that."

"I need to get out of here *now*."

"Well the front door magically disappeared, so how will you manage that?"

Sweat poured down his face. His hands were shaking like he

had a nervous condition. He glanced toward the door at the end of the hallway. "There's a—another door," he managed to say.

"Then go check it out."

"I don't think I can." Jeremy was frozen, his fight-or-flight instinct stuck on neutral.

Laney's voice insinuated itself into the soft tissue of his brain. "You need to move."

He placed a hand against the wall for support, his palm so sweaty it nearly slid right off.

"I can't."

"Take a deep breath."

Jeremy obeyed, hearing the wet intake of air as he sucked snot higher into his nose.

"Now let it out."

It spluttered out in a choked gust.

"Now move, goddamn you."

His feet carried him like an unwilling puppet down the hallway. He blinked sweat from his eyes, and a room abruptly, inexplicably appeared on his left. He screamed and made a half-assed evasive maneuver that ended with him colliding with the opposite wall.

The room was lightless, its walls tiled with some dark reflective surface. He leaned forward for a better look, trying to figure out what he was looking at, when an explosion of white light filled his vision, followed seconds later by the roar of static. He screamed again, but it was drowned in the chaos.

When Jeremy's voice cracked to silence, his throat tasting vaguely of blood, he stared through tear-filled eyes at a room filled with old televisions blaring static.

"What's going on?" Laney said.

He told her, his words barely coherent through the tremors in his voice.

"Go check it out."

Jeremy whined. He couldn't help himself. He was one scare away from pissing his pants. But, once again, his feet dragged him, puppet-like, into the next room. He was struck by the disturbing feeling that he was not entirely in control of his actions, but the thought quickly vanished as he leaned toward one of the screens and saw a face emerge through the static. It was a woman staring directly into the camera. A time stamp in the bottom right hand corner read a date only three weeks ago.

"Laney," Jeremy said. "When did the last victim go missing?"

"Sometime in the middle of last month. Why?"

"I think I'm looking at her."

"You found a body?"

"No, she's on one of the TV screens."

The girl, her chubby cheeks sheened in sweat, explained how she often woke up in the middle of the night thinking of the house —the house Jeremy was currently standing in he assumed—until one day she decided to check it out for herself. "It chose me," she said. "I went to it and here is my confession."

A second woman appeared on another television then another, followed by a middle-age man, until every set in the room showed a different face. They were all giving a similar confession.

A semblance of understanding entered Jeremy's mind, the pieces of an unknowable puzzle struggling vainly to fit together, the edges touching but not settling into place. He attempted to make sense of it anyway.

"We've got this all wrong," he said. "There's no serial killer. There isn't even a man. It's this place. It's luring people here."

Silence from Laney; Jeremy raised his eyebrows in anticipation of an answer. He was about to ask if she was still there, when the headset crackled and she said, "Whom do you think you've been talking to?" It wasn't her voice on the phone. Maybe it never had been. It didn't even sound like her. It was low, without inflection, and far away.

Ripping the headset from his ear, Jeremy chucked it blindly into the dark.

He was standing at the end of the hallway now, directly in front of the steel door. Glancing over his shoulder, he prayed for an exit, but a wall of televisions barred his path. Each contained a face making its own horrific confession.

Jeremy reached for the door handle, opened it. A shape moved in the next room. It was perched on a chair rigged with tubing and machinery.

A second movement out of the corner of his eye caught his attention. The walls were a confusion of rusted machinery and naked human bodies. Each of them moved feebly, their eyes closed, flesh penetrated by tubes, wires and shanks of metal, all of it dripping blood and condensation. He recognized some of the faces from the television room and vomited between his shoes.

The shape perched on the chair moved again.

As it closed the distance between them, Jeremy failed to make out anything familiar. It was like staring at an abstract sculpture given perverse life. Something cold and wet clamped over his mouth. He couldn't even scream as metal tubes pierced his chest, breaking ribs, and taking root in his organs.

It was his turn to confess.

SEX TOYS

After taking a concoction of sex enhancing drugs and detouring through a maze of alleys and parking lots, Bodie, Aisling and Emily arrived at the derelict pet shop, and Bodie switched on his camcorder.

Squinting through the viewfinder, he saw a close-up of the front door, its wire glass window veined with cracks. He fingered back the zoom. The building's façade was a sun-sapped yellow. Paint had flaked off in places to reveal the porous concrete underneath. A faded, illegible sign hung above the display window, which was broken and boarded up with graffitied sheets of plywood.

In the distance behind the shop loomed the jagged silhouette of factories and towers belching smoke into the indigo sky: an image conjured by a German Expressionist, a nightmare of shadows and sharp angles. It was beautiful. Bodie thought it would make a great establishing shot.

"You sure this place isn't going to fall down on top of us?"

Bodie turned toward Emily's voice. Both she and Aisling wore corsets and short black skirts studded with metal hardware and fish net stockings. Other than having identical costumes, they looked nothing alike. Emily's hair was black and Aisling's bleached white. Emily was also heavier, her uniformly pale skin plump around the stomach and breasts, which burst from her corset as if starving for release. Aisling on the other hand was almost skeletally thin, her cheekbones hoarding the day's growing shadows.

Emily pulled up her corset, re-adjusting it over her ample breasts. She said, "I hate to interrupt your previs jackoff, but are you sure we won't be crushed to death as soon as we step inside that door?"

"Relax. I scouted the place last week. It's safe."

"What about the toys?" Aisling asked. She was referring to the living sex toys they had ordered on the black market. They were grown in a basement by an amateur scientist and designed to resemble small, portly creatures with various animal traits.

"Props, not toys," Bodie amended.

Emily rolled her eyes.

"The guy said they were inside. This is the place we decided on."

"They better be," Emily said. "Those things cost a fortune."

"I trust him. He's never given me a reason not to," Bodie said, turning back to face the pet shop. "Let's head inside. I don't want to be shooting this goddamn thing all night."

He started toward the door, gave the handle a hard pull and walked inside. The room was dark, but the light from the open doorway provided a murky grey glow that gave the scene an unsettling beauty.

There was little evidence that it had once been a pet shop. A rusted birdcage in the corner, an overturned shelf, and broken fish tanks were the only relics of its past function. Otherwise the place was littered with garbage and debris.

He held the camcorder up to his face and panned from left to right and back again, lingering over every broken bottle, used condom, and discarded needle with a pornographer's gusto. Bodie breathed heavily, excited. The vision that had been percolating in his brain for weeks was about to come to life.

Once shooting and editing were complete, Bodie would have a total of twelve short films, enough for a multimedia exhibit at the local art gallery. He planned to have one flat screen television for each short mounted to the walls. They would be widely spaced and divided with moveable office walls. The overhead lights would be dim, almost non-existent, while a second set positioned low to the ground and aimed slightly upwards would produce deformed, elongated shadows whenever the gallery's visitors passed in front of them. The overall effect would be of walking through a dimly lit cave with isolated windows into different regions of Bodie's twisted imagination. His own carefully constructed hell.

Spotting something, he moved across the floor to the back of the room, broken glass crunching underfoot.

"Hey girls, get over here. I think I found our props."

He pointed at a crinkled blue tarp. It bulged in several places, hinting at the irregular shapes underneath.

As she approached, Emily said, "Oh my fucking God, what is that smell?"

Bodie took in a lung full of air through his nose and his face contorted with worry. He took one edge of the tarp and yanked it away. Its crackling was amplified by the emptiness of the room. Emily groaned.

Underneath were three decomposing, child-sized bodies. Their skin was black with rot and covered in whitish-green mucus. Two out of the three had potbellies and stubby, toddler-like limbs, while the third looked more like a fish, its body flat and diamond-shaped. But the strangest feature of all was their heads. Each had the deformed head of a dinosaur.

Aisling spun around and puked loudly.

Bodie turned in time to catch the second gush of vomit jetting yellow and thick from her mouth. It hit the floor with a splash, adding to the overall griminess of the place. She retched and squeezed out one final, diminished stream of bile and stomach acid before sawing an arm over her lips.

"Your guy gave us broken toys," she said in a pathetic childish voice.

Emily threw her hands up in the air. "Goddamnit. I wanted to fuck a toy that didn't smell like road kill, is that too much to ask?"

She went over to Aisling and started rubbing her back.

Bodie said. "We can make this work."

"Fuck you. Aisling can't even stand the smell of them. How do you expect her to give a performance?"

"She'll be fine. Her role is minimal."

Finger-combing the flecks of vomit from Aisling's hair, she said, "How about we find your guy and kick him in the kidneys until he pisses blood? He sold us corpses for fuck sake. I doubt the pheromones even work anymore."

"Listen," Bodie raised an imploring hand. "We can make this work. The rotting flesh might add something extra to the film." He gave an ironic shrug, squinting his eyes and scrunching up his face as he realized the morbidity of his words.

Emily laughed. It was sharp and humorless.

"We paid good money for toys we could fuck. Your job was to capture that moment on camera. That's why we're here. That's why we took the drugs."

"C'mon, Emily, you've done much weirder stuff before. Just give it a shot. If nothing else, you get to add something fucked up to your little black book of perversions."

He'd hit the right nail on the head. Emily softened and seemed to consider his proposal. Then, finally, she said, "I'll make you a deal."

"What's that?" Bodie's voice carried the hint of a smile.

"We'll shoot your stupid film, but Aisling's role has to be kept to a minimum, and when we get out of here we're going to find your guy and get our money back."

"Well, let's not waste anymore time."

He pointed with a black lacquered fingernail to the corner with the birdcage.

"Emily, lie down over there," and turning to Aisling he handed her the camcorder.

Bodie picked up one of the toys and hugged it close to his chest, as though it were still alive and starved for warmth. Small anthropoids the size of lice or fleas could be seen milling about the slime coating its flesh, their tiny mandibles working as they fed. The toy's milky blue eye stared directly at him, the predatory slash of a slitted pupil still visible through death's cataract.

The toy and camcorder exchanged hands. Aisling now held the

corpse in a loose, reluctant grip. She gagged once, her eyes welling with tears, and turning her head, spit several times on the floor.

"Doing okay?" Bodie asked.

Aisling stuck out her studded tongue at him.

"When I call action I want you to walk over to Emily, bend down so the camera gets a good look at your ass, and hand over the prop."

He turned to Emily, who had cleared away the filth from her spot in the corner and now lay in an awkward Venus pose. "When you have it in your arms, I want you to fondle it, rub it against your body, and, if you're feeling adventurous, give it a good long lick."

He trained the camcorder on her and yelled, "Action."

Emily adopted a relaxed, licentious expression that had become her trademark in Bodie's films. She wriggled her body as if she couldn't contain the sexual energy building inside her.

Aisling entered the frame, cradling the toy in her arms. She too had gotten into character and no longer looked like she was holding a dead, rotting thing. Her grip was firm, sure, and the look on her face was one of playful sensuality. Her black, many-buckled boots carried her over to Emily, who reached up with eager fingers. The corpse sagged, boneless, as it transferred hands. Its mouth lolled open revealing a palate and tongue studded with jagged teeth.

Emily pressed the little body against her chest, smearing its cadaverine on her cleavage. The pale half-globes glistened wetly. She cupped the back of its head and pushed her fingers forward so that the jaws clamped shut, misting the air with yellow fluid. Using her other hand, Emily pressed into the creature's groin and slid her palm up its belly and over the twin mounds of its striving breasts. She stopped at its throat and gave it a gentle squeeze.

As she drew the toy's head closer to her face, her eyes took on a lazy look of lust. She stuck out her tongue. It was long and pointed and she could curl it almost under her chin. It hung in the air a moment, trembling with the effort it took to hold it out. Her throat moved as she swallowed. When her tongue finally made contact, her gag reflex engaged instantly and violently, but she lapped the slimy dead flesh anyway.

The camera zoomed into an extreme close-up just in time to catch a tether of saliva connecting Emily's tongue to the toy's face snap and dangle from her bottom lip.

Bodie yelled cut.

Emily spat the foulness from her mouth, and as she went to stand a loud bang issued from the opposite side of the room. She dropped back down, assuming the stance of a hunted animal.

Bodie spun in the direction of the sound. Two sheets of plywood—spray painted with a cryptic tag—covered a door-sized section of the wall. The bang resounded a second time and Body reached into his pocket for an antique stiletto he'd stolen during one of his B and E jobs. With the push of a button, the blade popped free and clicked into place.

"What was that?" Aisling said.

Bodie's knuckles turned white from clutching the knife.

"Probably a fucking hobo. I bet the piece of shit was watching us through a slit in the plywood, jerking off."

He advanced toward the plywood barrier.

"Don't be an idiot," Emily said.

Bodie put the knife between his teeth and started pulling at the plywood.

"Stop," Emily hissed.

The topmost piece of plywood came down with a rending of nails out of plaster and was followed seconds later by the bottom sheet, which simply collapsed to the floor, its nails so consumed by rust they couldn't even hold up its weight without the top sheet providing support. In their place stood a doorway into darkness so absolute it looked solid, like a slab of obsidian.

"This is our cue to nope-the-fuck-out-of-here," Emily said.

Bodie switched on the camera's light attachment, revealing a set of stairs leading down at a steep angle. The steps had been eaten away by damp and some kind of black mold. They descended into a region of the basement where even Bodie's powerful light could not penetrate. From the depths came a smell like someone dropped a truckload of rotten eggs into a vat of raw sewage. Bodie coughed and choked.

"What's wrong?" Aisling said.

Bodie held the camera at arm's length so that the light could reach a greater distance. He saw nothing but more stairs. Darkness pooled around the limits of the beam like an oil spill.

"Hey, homeless Joe, you want a sandwich?"

"C'mon Bodie," Aisling pleaded.

"I'm going down," he said. "If the hobo jumps me, I'll stab him in the face."

"Why won't you listen to me," Emily was screaming now. "I hope you get hurt you dumb fuck."

He ignored her, accustomed to the abuse, and put his foot on the first step. It sagged under his weight and gave way with a wet shredding sound. His feet shot out in front of him, and he landed hard on his ass, breaking the second step. Then he was sliding. A scream ripped from his throat. He tried to stop himself, but the steps were slick with rot and he couldn't get a handhold. It also didn't help that he was determined to hold on to the camera.

Light jounced off the stairs, walls and sloped ceiling as an esophageal darkness swallowed him whole. Finally, after a dizzying, back-bruising eternity, he hit the bottom.

Something in his ass cracked and a gush of anxiety flooded his gut. He patted himself with his free hand, searching for protruding bones or impaled splinters of wood. Thankfully he was unscathed except for torn and dirty jeans. The camera, too, by some miracle, was fine. The only evidence of his fall was the canted light attachment.

Bodie brushed wood splinters and sweat from his face, bent his head back and screamed toward the matchbook-sized light of the doorway.

"I'm okay. I think I broke my ass, though."

"Do you need help coming back up?" Emily's voice, distant yet amplified by the tunnel acoustics of the stairwell.

"I don't think so."

Grunting, he got first to his knees, then his feet and, reaching around, pulled his cellphone out of his back pocket. It was snapped almost in half, the pieces held together by a joint of circuitry. That explained the crack. He swore and stuffed the phone back into his pocket. The stiletto was nowhere in sight.

"Is anyone down there with you?" Emily called out.

Bodie squinted into the dark. The basement was silent except for the occasional far off drip of water. He raised the camera and panned the room. The crooked light revealed a scene that filled him with dread he did not understand. Dark, prehistoric plants—monstrous ferns, cycads and cypresses—sprouted from the raw concrete in dense, impenetrable thickets, their branches still and dripping moisture. Ivy and moss hung down from the ceiling, which receded into the darkness high above.

As he stared, taking in the primal, subterranean landscape, he managed to identify the source of his dread. It was some buried genetic memory tracing back through time when the progenitors of the human race were not yet at the pinnacle of the food chain. When the threat of predators and the fear of having one's flesh shredded between snarling, reeking jaws was all too real.

His fight-or-flight instinct kicked in, threatening to choke him, and yet he remained rooted to the spot, his eyes transfixed on the pool of light shed by the camera's attachment. The prehistoric flora stood unmoving, save the occasional glimmer of moisture sliding down their leaves. The tree line seemed to regard him with cold indifference, like an old god looking on a haphazard or whimsical creation—every ounce of his being cringed away from it. His balls tightened and his bowels churned cement.

None of this was real, he thought. It couldn't be real. The world was ravaged and insane, but this defied reason.

"Did you hear me?" Emily again.

The foliage stirred to Bodie's left. He jumped and reflexively shined the light in that direction. Two eyes, unnaturally far apart, reflected the light back.

Bodie made a garbled sound somewhere between a scream and a sob, turned around and started up the stairs at a run. Several steps threatened to surrender under his weight, but he managed to make it to the top without breaking his legs. The girls stared at him in mute anticipation.

"There's something down there," Bodie said. "We need to get the fuck out of here."

"Finally," Emily breathed.

As they moved toward the door there was a deafening roar from somewhere below. The floor heaved upwards as something heavy struck it from underneath. Bodie was thrown forward, his chin slamming hard against the linoleum. He bit down on his tongue and his mouth filled with blood. Then, with a tremendous crack, the hump in the middle of the room flattened to its original state. Plaster poured from the ceiling. Bodie turned his head in time to see a foot-long gap form between the baseboard and the floor. Splinters connected the divide like a row of sharp teeth. What he experienced next could only be compared to the breathless seconds of anticipation as a rollercoaster chugged to its greatest height and hung there suspended before whooshing back to earth. Only this sensation was glass-ridden with mortal terror.

Bodie slammed his eyes shut, thinking, we're dead... we're fucking dead. Whatever's living down there is going to eat us alive. The ground shook, the jolt sprung his eyes open, and he saw Emily reaching for the door handle. That's when the floor gave out below them. The sound was deafening, apocalyptic. None of them had time to scream. The prehistoric forest swallowed them into its stinking, salivating maw.

Emily blinked awake. She was lying in a pile of debris, and through the haze in her vision, she saw strange plants protruding from the mess—they seemed to belong to another time.

Every inch of her exposed skin stung from the myriad cuts and bruises suffered during her fall. Her face and arms were tacky with blood. Her ears rang and her head ached. Concussion, probably.

Her arms extended out, bracing in a push up position. She lifted her chest, spitting blood, shaking her head to clear it, dust and splinters flying from her hair, and staggered unevenly to her feet. A light stuttered to her right. She moved toward it, feeling as though she were wading through a dream. It was Bodie's camera.

She bent to pick it up and as the light swung toward the floor, she saw him. His neck was broken, the spinal cord punching through his flesh. Wide, terrified eyes stared up at Emily. They looked even worse in the broken, flickering light of the camera attachment. She reached for him, wanting to touch his skin one last time, but drew away trembling. She had to find Aisling.

She started to move, limping on what must have been a sprained ankle. Pushing ferns aside, she penetrated the rainforest, whispering Aisling's name into the silence. The sound felt unwelcome, as if the place were alive and sleeping.

After some time she came to a clearing in the jungle. On the concrete floor lay two withered corpses. They looked like human women, except for their faces, which tapered into primitive snouts. And their skin, though rotted, still held the suggestion of scales. Their legs were bent and open, stomachs once distended in pregnancy now shapeless and deflated. They wore rags and their skin was slathered in the same slime that coated the toys upstairs.

Emily squatted down and fingered something that protruded from one of the women's thighs. A claw, curved and tapered, black as ebony.

She stood again and limped dreamily back into the trees.

Hours seemed to pass before she reached another landmark. It was a pillbox bunker of crumbling, blood-sprayed concrete. Several loopholes gave onto the almost palpable darkness inside.

Emily approached and stabbed the light into one of the apertures. The air was thick with dust, motes swimming like plankton in the pallid beam. A folding steel table, coated in grime, stood against the far wall. It was paired with a rusting chair. There was also the suggestion of file cabinets in the corner, but the density of the bunker's gloom made it difficult to tell. Emily rounded the building and found a door. It was heavy and reinforced with cross bars. A gentle push was all it took for the door to open on its rotten hinges. She played the light over the walls and floor. A wide blood smear adorned both, dry and faded to a ruddy brown. No one had been here for years.

She took one step inside and froze. A shrill scream had rung out behind her. Emily turned to stare at the jungle, the moisture, the blackness. As she listened, the scream came again and this time it sounded closer. It was repeated several times and eventually morphed into words, or more precisely, one word. Her name repeated in a panicked staccato.

Aisling exploded from the trees, her mouth frozen in a terrified rictus. Blood plastered her hair to her scalp and ran down her face in murky rivulets. Her arms pumped madly and it took Emily a second to realize that her left arm was missing below the elbow. Well, not exactly. The joint trailed a limp tentacle of shredded meat. A severed tendon, white as uncooked fish, dangled from the ruined appendage, slapping grotesquely against her hip as she ran. Emily's gaze lowered to the deep claw marks running the length of Aisling's thighs. With a jolt, she remembered the corpses from the clearing, frozen eternally in postures of pregnancy, and the single predatory claw jutting from one of their legs. She imagined something inhuman, possibly reptilian, prying them open and pulling out the thing that slid wetly out—one of the creatures they'd found upstairs.

Maybe they weren't toys after all, she thought, but something unknown that had escaped their underground world to die on the surface. Her mind almost came undone. She could feel the wires fraying and spitting sparks.

All that was needed was one more push and she'd be irretrievably lost. That push came seconds later as Aisling approached, still screaming, her travesty of an arm slapping back and forth, back and forth, pendulum-like. It would have been lulling if it weren't so repulsive. But it wasn't Aisling that made Emily's mind snap like a tightly stretched violin string. It was the pair of eyes that appeared over Aisling's shoulder, glowing in the light of the camera—eyes that were too high and far apart to belong to anything human.

Emily let out a strangled cry. Her eyes bulged dumbly and a string of snot hung from one nostril. She was too far beyond reason to care.

The thing that bore down on Aisling was over eight feet tall, with a bipedal saurian body and incongruous human arms that nearly touched the ground. It was skinless, crimson muscle showing clearly through a web of yellow veins and white sinew. Its skull tapered into a snout that split into a smile filled with crooked teeth. The eyes above it were milky blue and apparently blind. Emily had the sudden intuition that it relied on its sense of smell to capture prey. Its tail was broken and dragged limply behind it.

One of its clawed hands swung out. Blood sprayed. Aisling was thrown face first on the hard concrete. Her scream faltered, but only for a moment. As she struggled to get up it resumed at a new and higher octave.

The saurian-thing placed one foot on the small of Aisling's back and applied pressure until Emily heard a crunch that made her flinch. Aisling stopped screaming. Her limbs jerked and a puddle of urine spread out under her. The saurian-thing squatted on backward knees, encompassed the back of Aisling's head with one hand, and tore it off her shoulders in one effortless thrust. Her spinal cord came with it, sliding out of its fleshy casing. The thing held up its prize, fingering the dripping vertebra with its free hand. It uttered a few incomprehensible syllables while staring into Aisling's sightless eyes before turning its attention on Emily.

She dropped the camera and ran. Blindly. Madly. Screaming. Voiding herself as she went. The thing's heavy footfalls pounded the concrete behind her. She plunged into the jungle, trees whipping her face and marking her cheeks with sharp, bloody kisses. She was going to die here, savagely torn apart. She wondered, insane with fear, whether Aisling's brain stayed alive long enough for her eyes to see her headless body prone on the concrete.

She ran, heedless of the pain in her ankle. Darkness pressed against her eyes. She could hear the saurian thing's heavy breathing behind her. She broke off to the left, increasing her speed despite the exhaustion stealing over her body.

The breathing receded; the thing was losing pace. She continued to run, her lungs ready to burst, her throat full of phlegm and fiery pain.

Then came a splash and coolness around her ankles. Water. She stopped, listened. She couldn't hear the creature anymore. It was gone.

A trembling wreck from the adrenaline, she bent down, her

panting coming out in eerie little moans, like something one would hear in a madhouse. She twirled her fingers through the water, totally insensate now. One of her eyes was twitching, and her lower lip protruded, wet with saliva. She had been clenching her teeth so hard one of them had loosened. She stank of sweat, urine and shit. In no time, this place had reduced her to something mindless and feral.

If she was sane enough, she would have found a way to end her own life, but her shattered mind refused even to let her do that. All she could do was twirl her fingers in the icy water and stare off into the perpetual night.

A wave struck her hand, followed by another. Something was moving out there. How large was this body of water? Was it some kind of underground lake? She straightened into a standing position and looked out to where she supposed the wave originated. The water hissed and seethed as something huge displaced it, heading toward shore.

Toward her.

Emily was riveted to the spot. Perhaps her body was finally surrendering to death. As the thing in the water approached, the waves lapping against Emily's legs grew stronger, and she could smell it now, a rich yeasty tang combined with rotting meat. The waves relaxed. She heard the scrape of sand as the unseen hulk beached itself in shallower waters. Its breath was hot against her face. She heard a wet peeling sound, followed by a hiss, which could have only been the creature opening its impossibly huge jaws.

A FEAST OF YOU

1. The Road Out

Ryker looked at the sky reflected in his coffee. Thick iron clouds pushed in from the city he had just fled, moving toward the diner with almost predatory purpose. He shifted uneasily in his booth. Cracked and blistered vinyl creaked under his weight. He brought the mug to his lips and drank. His hand shook so badly, a thread of coffee dribbled from the corner of his mouth. It was scalding, but he barely noticed. The only thought that occupied his mind was how he needed to get as far away from the city as possible. And as soon as the caffeine kicked in, he couldn't afford to waste another minute. He was, after all, still within their zone of influence.

Despite its stinging warmth, the coffee—straight black and electrified with three packs of sugar—did an excellent job jump-starting his system. He hadn't slept in over forty-eight hours and the energy now easing into his bloodstream almost brought tears to his eyes. The only thing was, he also had very little to drink in the last couple days and the coffee was beginning to fill his bladder to the point of discomfort. An itinerary formed in his mind. He'd take a piss, finish his third cup, leave the diner, drive until nightfall, find a cheap motel, unplug the room's electronics to prevent them from learning of his whereabouts, get a good night sleep and finish up the drive in the morning. There was bound to be someplace where they couldn't find him. He hoped with every quivering nerve in his body that it wasn't simply a pipe dream.

The bell above the door jangled. Ryker spun around so fast his neck cracked. A family of three stood in the entrance. They looked like they'd stepped from the pages of a department store catalogue. The father had a kind but plain face, balding, the dark hair on his temples turning grey. He wore a t-shirt with the logo of some sports team Ryker remembered from his childhood. His wife was a head shorter, also plain but beautiful in her way. A scarf was knotted loosely around her neck and a purse dangled form one arm. She held her daughter's hand, the diamond on her ring finger catching and refracting the diner's fluorescent light. The child was clad in bright colors and in her other hand she carried a plastic, zipped container decorated with leering cartoon characters.

Sweat popped on Ryker's forehead and trickled down the groove of his spine. An invisible fist punched through his stomach and squeezed his entrails. For a moment, he couldn't breathe, couldn't move. He watched, riveted with terror, as the father inclined his head, said something to his daughter that made her laugh, and together the family made their way to a booth on the opposite side of the diner. The only other patron apart from Ryker, an older man with a grey beard and weatherworn jacket, smiled at the little girl as she passed.

Ryker tore his eyes away from the new arrivals. The clouds reflected in his coffee were closer now. He scooted to the edge of his seat, shot up and walked briskly to the bathroom. His bladder was so full it hurt, and for one embarrassed second he thought he'd pissed himself, but it was only sweat. It coated every inch of his body like an amniotic sack.

The bathroom door hit the wall with a thunderclap smash. He darted toward the urinal, fumbled with his fly, and let loose a stream so powerful it splashed back from the stained porcelain. He bowed his head, breath coming out in labored gasps. His heart hammered, gunfire-quick. Empty, he zipped up, and staggered to the sink. His long black hair was plastered to his forehead. He threw cold water in his face, made a sound crossed between a groan and a whisper. *That family...they're just people...they're harmless.* Even so, they reminded Ryker too much of them—those *things* he'd fled from.

He remained at the sink for another minute or two, hands grasping the edges, head bent toward the drain. When his heart rate slowed and his breathing grew steady, he straightened and exited the bathroom.

The family, the old man and the waitress behind the counter all stared at him. His throat moved. He directed his gaze at the floor. Quick, purposeful strides carried him back to his booth. He gripped the handle of his coffee mug in a quaking fist and downed the rest of its contents, wincing at a bitter taste he hadn't noticed before. When he turned around, running a hand over his mouth, the waitress was standing inches from his face.

"Ready to settle up?" she asked.

"Y-yeah," he managed to stutter, removing the wallet from his back pocket.

He threw a five on the chipped Formica and got the hell out of there. He had to move.

The engine of his rusted beater growled in protest before sputtering to life. He peeled out of the gravel parking lot, throwing up dust and hitting the highway at sixty miles an hour. The woods on either side blurred into abstraction, flashes of green, brown and grey as the sky leaked through between gaps in the trees.

When the diner shrank then disappeared in the rearview mirror, Ryker finally eased off the gas. The speedometer swung from one-twenty to ninety. *Thankfully this piece of shit didn't explode* —and he couldn't help but laugh. It was strained but genuine, and the longer it went on, the louder and more unhinged it became. Soon he was howling, tears blurring his vision, an open palm beating a crazed rhythm against the ceiling. Calm returned in waves until he was silent and staring at the road, his throat and chest sore from the outburst.

Silence reigned for a time before he decided to turn on the radio. *It should be safe to listed to a couple songs*, he reasoned. As long as he remained quiet, they wouldn't be able to hear him over the airwaves.

The jockey said, "Now here's a favorite of mine. I think many of you out there can use some of its medicine—especially with all the bad in the world lately. So here's—"

Ryker relaxed his shoulders, easing back into his seat, allowing the music to wash over him. The drum beat a slow, heavy sound. The guitar was mellow and muted, the lyrics deep-voiced and lullaby-smooth. Combined with the monotony of the road, the flashing yellow lines, Ryker felt himself lulled into a trance-like state. His eyelids grew heavy, his muscles slack.

A flash in the rearview mirror. He shook his head to clear it. Another flash and Ryker recognized it for what it was: lightening. The clouds and the storm they carried were closing in.

His head was full of cotton, his eyelids dropped and his limbs were growing numb. *What the hell is happening?* He blinked several times, but his vision refused to clear. It was like his eyes were smeared with petroleum jelly. He pulled onto the side of the road and could only tell he was on the shoulder by the crunch of gravel under the tires. His eyes were useless and he could barely keep them open.

His breathing grew shallower by the second, the rise and fall of his chest a lulling rhythm. *Oh shit. No. I can't fall asleep now. What's going on?* He lifted a leaden arm and clumsily jabbed the button to turn off the radio. Silence except for his own breathing. Thunder rumbled not far behind. His eyelids fluttered closed, his head lolled onto one shoulder. *Please. Don't fall asleep.* The plea crawled around inside his head. As he plunged into a mire of unconsciousness his last thought was of the strange bitterness in his last mouthful of coffee.

2. Family

He woke to the familiar smell of his pillow and the comforting swaddle of bed sheets. Opening his eyes, he glimpsed a white ceiling dappled with luminous stickers of stars and planets. Because it was daytime, the stickers refused to glow, offering instead a dull and sickly yellow. Rolling his head to one side, Ryker saw a dresser with red and blue drawers. A row of junior sports trophies shone atop it. He glanced in the opposite direction: open dinosaur-patterned curtains, bars on the window. The fragrance of a vanilla scented candle wafted from beneath the closed bedroom door.

The realization of his whereabouts came with a sickening, icy dread. He tried to sit up. Metal clanged against metal and he was yanked back down into a prone position. Handcuffs, tethered to steel rails on either side of the mattress, were clamped to his wrists.

He screamed, curses and spittle flying from his lips. A ringing clamor filled the room as he fought against his restraints. They'd found him. His attempt at escape had failed.

Beneath the din of his struggle, Ryker heard another sound. Footsteps from somewhere down the hall. *Oh shit, they're coming.* Closer now. He could just make out a shadow under the door. The knob turned with agonizing slowness. Then the door opened.

She stood on the threshold in a sundress, smiling at him. A tray topped with a sandwich and glass of water rested in French-manicured hands.

"Please keep it down, James. Your sister is trying to do her homework."

Mother moved across the room and placed the tray on the bedside table. She sat down beside Ryker, took the knife and fork positioned to either side of the plate and meticulously sliced the sandwich into bite-size pieces. Stabbing one of the squares with the fork, she brought it to Ryker's lips, but he moved his head away.

"We're not angry with you, James," she said in her oddly musical voice. "But, you've upset us. Deeply."

Ryker said nothing, only stared.

"Now, please. Eat your lunch, honey. You need the energy. Tonight is important."

"I'm not hungry."

"Don't be silly. I'm your mother. I know you're hungry."

Ryker wanted to tell her to shove the sandwich up her ass, but he knew that would only bring him pain. And she was right: he *was* starving. He needed food. His stomach was a growling void. He felt weak, barely alive.

With a stab of defeat, he opened his mouth. Mother's eyes widened, too wide, the lids peeling back unnaturally as though forced open with a speculum. She moved the piece of sandwich into Ryker's mouth. His lips closed over the tines and Mother slowly pulled the utensil out.

"That's good," she said. "You need to stay strong. Your little adventure must have taken a lot out of you."

He chewed, remained silent. *Not my little adventure*, he thought, *what about what came before that, the whole reason why I ran away? You don't think that drained my energy, you stupid, selfish bitch?*

She smiled wider. "Like I said, James, we're not angry with you. I had a talk with your father and he knows exactly what's going through your head. It's one of those *phases*. The wanderlust that comes to every young adult who dreams of leaving the nest." A laugh. "If you didn't stop for coffee, you may just have slipped us a little longer. But our reach is long, James. We found the diner and dropped a little concoction—my own recipe—into that cheap coffee. You didn't stand a chance but you knew that before you decided to run away from us."

"I can't do this anymore," Ryker said. The words tumbled out in a hushed tone.

Mother shushed him and placed a hand on his cheek. Lifting the glass of water, she brought it to his lips. He drank greedily, water running down his chin and chest.

When he finished drinking, he struggled to catch his breath. Mother put down the glass and leaned forward until their brows were almost touching.

"I want you to understand something. No, I *need* you to understand something, James. Death and treason tore our kind apart. It's only us left. And we have to stick together, be there for one another. You can't run away. You can't leave us, James, because we need you. Do you understand?"

Scalding tears gushed from Ryker's eyes. He nodded weakly.

"Good," Mother said patting his wet cheek. "Very good."

"I'm sorry," Ryker blubbered. He couldn't help it. The scars carved deep inside him compelled apology.

"You will stay in your room until tonight. Then we'll organize a family meeting and make things right again. In the meantime, get some rest and think about what you've done."

Mother stood up, reached into the pocket of her sundress and produced a key. She used it to unlock the handcuff on Ryker's left wrist, the one farthest from the bedside table.

"Now you can eat and drink on your own. But no fooling around. You don't want to anger your father."

She nodded once, apparently satisfied he wouldn't try anything stupid, and left the room. As soon as the door closed, Ryker threw himself at the sandwich and stuffed the meal into his mouth, snorting like a starved animal. He swallowed painfully, nearly choking, and washed everything down with another sloppy drink of water. The glass drained, he replaced it on the tray and lay back down.

What now? Ryker had never attempted to escape before and feared he'd spoiled his only chance. His family had likely taken every precaution so that he wouldn't slip from their grasp again. And with that thought came the realization that life at home would be a lot worse now than it had been already. He didn't think he could bear it any longer. His eyes went to the knife on the dinner tray. He picked it up, tested its weight.

All he had to do was plunge it into his throat or chest. An image came to his mind's eye: the glinting steel of the knife disappearing into folds of flesh under his jawline; a dark pulse of arterial blood pumping then spraying a mad Rorschach on the sterile white walls. The visual made him cringe, but he raised the point to the pulse at his throat.

It will only hurt for a minute.

He applied more pressure. A stinging sensation as the tip of the blade bit through skin, drawing blood that coursed down and pooled on the ridge of his clavicle. Breath hissed through his teeth. He had to be quick. One hard stab would do the job.

He couldn't do it.

The air escaped his lungs in a rush of defeat. He dropped the knife on the table, sprawled on the bed. He was too cowardly for suicide. The howling oblivion of death was too terrifying to contemplate, especially when he considered that his family could follow him to the other side, and somehow pull him back. The more he thought about it, the more he came to accept that escape was impossible.

Having run out of options, Ryker closed his eyes and tried to sleep.

3. Void

He dreamed the house was moving. Floating through liquid darkness. Spinning end over end, yet all the furniture and decorations remained in their respective places. Dream logic informed him the house was traveling into a starless pocket between galaxies.

During its travels, familiar planets had soared past and were rapidly swallowed by the star-flecked blackness of space. Later, celestial bodies outside of human knowledge had emerged out of the unknown. The event horizon of a black hole glowed with a spectral light. And a vast mechanical construct had threatened to ensnare the house using some form of vestigial limb. But the house was protected and glided easily beyond its grasp. At the end of its journey there was a flash of prismatic light, followed by a seismic trembling, as the house floated on the edge of known reality.

For Ryker the trip was disorienting, dominated by a sensation like falling sideways into a lightless well. He experienced it as one divorced from their body, without the accompanying vertigo or nausea. The disorientation was more profound than that, a trembling on the level of consciousness and identity, something a person would feel in the throes of a psychotic episode. But Ryker was in control of his mind, or at least he felt that way in the dream, and was able to quiet his anxiety when an ordinary person would have fallen into gibbering insanity.

He climbed out of bed, no longer bound by the handcuffs, and walked to the window. He stared out, pressed his hand against the glass. It was cool to the touch. Outside, the darkness pulsed, pushing past his eyes and filling his head like water from a subterranean spring. He let the darkness fill him until it wore his skin like a raiment. The beat of his heart had faded into silence so acute it made his eardrums throb. He narrowed his eyes, trying to discern the exterior landscape, and saw nothing but the howling blackness beyond the stars.

Then he spotted movement. A shape too large for his mind to comprehend, something blind that regarded the house as it floated like a particle of dust through the crushing darkness. For all he knew, he was only looking at a small fraction of the whole thing—perhaps only a flake of dead skin falling from its body.

The house continued to drift and soon a more concrete form materialized out the void. At first it was nothing but a burgundy speck with a twinkling indigo core. Then it grew larger and took on a more intricate shape. It resembled a titan of interstellar dust and gas, yet at the same time it was unlike anything Ryker had seen in deep space photographs. It seemed to be alive. Its vast surface throbbed with unspeakable breath. It lumbered, unaware of the house's presence, and from its swirling flesh came the sound of musical piping. Ryker watched it, enthralled, and as he did so, something slammed into the opposite side of the glass.

He staggered back and almost fell. When he recovered, he was staring into the incomprehensible face of some being. Huge elephantine ears extended from either side of its head, which puckered in a vaguely rectal orifice. From it, a second face emerged like a spheroid tumor. It was devoid of feature save a grin filled with small, round teeth. The being snapped its jaws at the glass. Its massive, worm-like body trailed off into the void, tethered—umbilical-like—to some half-glimpsed, planet-sized monstrosity in the distance.

4. Board Game

Ryker woke with a gasp. Sister was perched on the edge of the bed, waving a board game above her head. The box was worn and sun-faded, the corners rubbed down to white. The bottom was stained to a dark brown. Pieces clattered like old broken bones inside.

"Want to play with me?" she asked.

She was four years younger than his eighteen, blonde like Mother, with anemic skin and a boy's physique. Her hair was greasy and knotted. A stale odor like old dough wafted from her body and permeated the room. She placed the box on the bed covers and crawled up beside Ryker, frowning.

"Is that blood? Are you bleeding?"

At first he didn't understand what she was talking about. Then he remembered holding the knife to his throat, contemplating the end. He shook his head. "It's nothing. I was being clumsy."

He grunted into a sitting position, looked down. A snake-stain of blood marred the bed sheet. His head hummed as he stared at it, forcing him to look away.

Sister giggled, a sound like razor blades against Ryker's eardrum. "Typical James. The clumsy dope."

She crossed her legs, threw the board game lid over her shoulder and unfolded the play area between them. It was a simple grid of squares against a yellow background. Unidentifiable stains slashed its rippled, warped surface. Sister reached back into the box and removed the other components. She dropped them with a wet splat on the game board: a bright pink bird fetus, a human tooth, petrified animal shit and various small cuts of viscera, still oleaginous with dark blood and serous fluid.

Wiping her hands on her pants, Sister said, "What are you? Base or Donian?"

Ryker frowned. "You're giving me a choice for once?"

She usually had her way, and always picked Donian, the pawns embodying the foundations of the universe. Which, invariably, left Ryker with Base: the noise or junk of creation.

She looked at him, waited for his answer.

"Well, in that case, I choose Donian."

He picked up the bird fetus, human tooth and one lump of viscera—*brown and corrugated, likely a shred of large intestine*, he thought—and placed them on his side of the board.

"I knew you would do that," Sister said, picking up the fossilized shit and remaining bits of organ. "It doesn't matter who I play. I'm still going to win."

Ryker abruptly realized he could steer the game in his favor. It didn't have to be a mindless diversion, but a means to an end, however small.

"What are we playing for?" he asked.

Sister placed a finger to her lip, thinking. "If I win," she said, tapping her front teeth with a fingernail, "I can have the heart."

A grin split her face, chapped lips peeling back to reveal a mouth populated by both baby and permanent teeth. The effect was grotesquely juvenile. Ryker remembered how Sister hated pulling out her teeth. They would often hang limply from the nerve, going black with decay before Mother and Father were required to hold her down and extract them by force. One such tooth was visible now, wagging like a loose shingle under the probing of her tongue.

Ryker shuddered. *The heart*, he thought, *she wants the heart*. She had always been a spiteful brat and this request only further reinforced Ryker's conviction. Sure, it made sense on the surface—the heart was the best part—but coming from his sister it was offensive and disrespectful. Ryker wondered if she possessed anything other than ill manners. The chances were slim. She spent her entire life sheltered and coddled by Mother and Father, who were willfully blind to the faults in her behavior. Because of this she acted purely out of abandon, heedless of the world outside her own whims.

"Fine," Ryker said, his voice laced with venom. "If I win, you have to unlock these handcuffs." He rattled them demonstratively against the rail jutting from the side of the bed. "I know you can. Key or no key."

Sister blew air out her mouth. It made a rude, flatulent sound.

"Yeah, right," she said.

"Do you seriously think I'm going to run away, again? I'm pretty sure our parents put measures into place to prevent that from happening. My wrist just hurts and my arm is starting to go numb."

Sister stared but offered no response, so Ryker continued, "I fucked up. Badly. I promise I won't ever do it again. I was just confused. Overwhelmed. I was suffocating and needed to get out for a little while. Clear my head."

"There's nothing to be confused about," Sister said. "Mother and Father provide us with everything we need. Do you even know how much you hurt them by leaving?"

Ryker let his chin drop to his chest. "I know. Like I said, I fucked up. I'm sorry."

"That's not going to cut it, Brother," Sister said darkly. "We're a close family and you don't seem to appreciate everything we have. How much we all love you."

The comment elicited weak laughter from Ryker. "It has nothing to do with love," he said, but in his mind he was uncertain whether he was conveying his feelings truthfully. He loved his family. He had no doubt of that. But part of him doubted they all shared the same definition of love. In recent years, Ryker had come to believe his family's love was little more than blind need for his companionship. Which, in some perverse way, transformed his desire to strike out on his own a personal attack against their support and goodwill. Of course, that wasn't true. Because of their tumultuous history, however, communicating these thoughts to his family was nearly impossible. It didn't fit their narrow conception of family life. He communicated none of this to his sister, though. Instead he said, "I didn't run away because I don't love you guys. I do, more than anything. It was a lapse of judgment. Nothing more. No point overthinking it."

Sister eyed him warily. After a lengthy pause in which they stared into the other's faces, she said, "You have a lot of work to do. I'll unlock you, but if you try anything, I'm going to make your life miserable."

There was no exaggeration in the threat. Ryker could see the conviction in her eyes. Black and glittering, like those of a carrion crow.

"I promise. I won't do it, ever again," Ryker said.

Sister curled all her fingers into a fist, except one. The pinky. It stuck out between them like a lifeline. "Pinky swear?" she asked.

Ryker curled his pink around hers. "Pinky swear," he said.

The game lasted nearly an hour. The siblings sat hunched over the board, attentions rapt, moving their pieces with strategic premeditation. For some time, Sister was winning. Every pawn she consumed from Ryker's forces was removed from play with a silent, cunning smile. Then, toward the final phase of the game, Ryker stole the advantage. He caught Sister off her guard, perhaps momentarily blinded by her arrogance, and devoured two of her pieces in a single advantageous stroke. She swore loudly and slammed her fist into the mattress. She didn't quite know it then, but her lapse had cost her the game. And two turns later, her last piece was swept from the board, leaving Ryker the victor.

Ryker laughed. It was brittle but genuine. "I win. For once," he said.

"Fuck that," Sister spat. "I'm not unlocking your handcuffs."

This didn't surprise Ryker. Sister was, after all, a sore loser. "Think about all the time I gave in whenever I lost. All the shit I owed you."

Color had risen in Sister's cheeks. The oil on her forehead glistened with a new patina of sweat. She held out her right hand, the fingers spread. "Fine, you bitch," she said.

From under the nail on her index finger emerged a needle-thin protuberance of bone. She pushed the game board out of the way resentfully, took hold of Ryker's forearm and inserted the bone growth into the keyhole in the handcuffs. She rotated her wrist once, twice. There was a dry click and the cuffs sprang loose.

Ryker pulled his hand away as if from an open flame, rubbing at the bones of his wrist.

"You have to admit, it was a good game," Ryker said.

"Fuck you."

5. Bathroom

When Sister left his room, Ryker dozed again, only this time his sleep was shallow and dreamless. When he woke, he felt even more rundown than before. He refused to lift his head from the pillow, refused to even open his eyes. His consciousness dipped in and out of a superficial puddle of sleep. Then he detected another presence in the room and opened his eyes. He sat up and saw Father standing at the foot of the bed.

"How are you?" he asked.

He was shorter than Ryker, his head balding in a wide strip from brow to crown. Square-rimmed glasses with thick lenses balanced on a nose reddened with burst capillaries. His arms were crossed over his chest.

"I'm okay," Ryker said. His voice was thin and husky with sleep.

"I thought Mother left one of the handcuffs still attached?"

"Sister unlocked it. It was the winning condition of our game. The thing was becoming painful."

Father nodded in slow faint motions, and then took in an audible rush of breath. "You didn't hurt yourself out there, did you?" He was talking about the world beyond their front door.

"No. I'm fine. The whole experience just tired me out."

"It'll do that," he said. "The outside wasn't meant for us. Not for extended periods of time, anyway."

Ryker nodded, recalling the exhaustion he'd felt while sitting in the diner, desperately trying to fill his body with caffeine. On the heels of that memory came the realization that he needed to use the bathroom. His bladder was full and was starting to hurt the same way it had at the diner.

He began to speak, hesitated. Then finally said, "Would it be okay if I used the washroom?"

"You can use the portable urinal."

"I can't leave my bedroom?"

"Not yet. We're not taking—"

"Where am I going to go?"

Father watched him through the magnifying lenses of his glasses.

"Wait for me here," Ryker said. "I'm going to piss my pants. I just have to use the washroom. I'll be right back."

"Be quick," Father said, after a pause. "I'll be right here."

Ryker scooted to the edge of the bed, allowed his legs to dangle over the edge for a minute as blood flowed back into them, and stood up. As he passed Father on his way out the door, he clamped a hand on his shoulder. Ryker wasn't sure what he meant by the gesture: reassurance, affection or camaraderie, but whatever the intention, Ryker felt a pang of emptiness.

In the bathroom, he emptied himself and took a long look in the mirror. Faintly, he could hear music coming from somewhere outside. A woman's voice, high and operatic. It was likely a piece from Mother's record collection. He ran the tap, filled his cupped hands, then splashed his face. Water ran down his skin in runnels and dripped into the basin. His breath splattered droplets against the mirror. He needed to get out of this place. He couldn't allow failure to dissuade him from a future attempt.

There was an exit nearby. He would make one more attempt to run away. All he had to do was exit the bathroom, make his way down the hall, open the door there and lock it behind him. He didn't know where it would take him, but it was worth a shot. Even if his parents had put measures into place to ensure his captivity, he was certain he could find a way to overcome them. After all, he'd already done it once before.

"One more try," he whispered and took a deep breath.

Carefully, quietly, he opened the bathroom door. It was silent, the hinges in good order. The music heightened in volume. It was indeed opera, but of a sinister sort. The singer's ominous melody was accompanied by the snarls of horns and the cries of violins. Thankfully, it was loud enough to mask Ryker's steps across the hardwood floor. Even so, he moved slowly, ensuring not to make the boards groan under his weight. On his way down the hallway, he passed the living room, where the music originated. He turned his head and chanced a look.

Mother stood by the record player. She appeared caught between one shape and another. Her head nearly touched the ceiling. A dark aura pulsed from her skin. She reached out to lift the needle, and Ryker saw her fingers were long and sharpened to points. He'd only seen her like this once before, when he was a child. His reaction now was the same as it had been then: raw, undiluted terror. He took a step back. A board creaked under him.

She turned her too-wide face in his direction. And he ran.

6. Outside

At the end of the hallway, he swung the door open. His foot snagged on the transition strip, throwing him into the space beyond. His palms scraped wet asphalt. Pain shuddered through his bones. He didn't know what he was expecting to find—a hallway, an alcove, another room—but it certainly wasn't an alley strewn with trash and the putrid carcasses of worms. Their bodies were long and string-thin, with skin the color of a urine-soaked diaper. A single black blemish, like a cycloptic eye, jeweled their spade-shaped heads. As he hung there, arms extended in a quivering push-up position, Ryker realized the worms were moving. The motion was slight, almost imperceptible, as though they were breathing weak, terminal breaths through their skin.

Ryker rolled on his back and sat up. Blood from his shredded elbows trickled down his forearms and wove crimson bracelets around his wrists. He was in the middle of extracting a pebble of glass from his hand, when he heard the click of the lock.

He was trapped— wherever this was.

The place was silent. No wind sighed. No thunder rumbled. The natural bustle and ambience of traffic was absent. It was so quiet Ryker's ears were ringing. He slowly, cautiously rose to his full height, casting a look round the alley for any signs of threat—

nothing but worms, their bodies splashed everywhere like a carpet of living angel hair pasta. Looking up, he saw a grey sky pregnant with storm. His mind flashed back on the seemingly interminable potential of the highway, stretching forever toward a life of freedom. A pang struck his chest. He forced the daydream into a mental shredder.

As he ventured down the narrow passage, he noticed a series of objects—traps of some kind—arrayed along the walls. Tiny, black cubes bleeding a fluorescent green powder. Mother and Father must have been here, armed the place against the infesting threat of the worms.

Emerging from the alley, Ryker found himself on an empty street. The lamps were dark husks. All the buildings were constructed of dull grey brick. The windows were smothered in dust. Nowhere could he see a poster or billboard to lend the place any personality. Even the traffic signage was sapped of color. And of course, there were no people. No birds flitting from lamppost to awning. No life anywhere.

What the hell is this place? He knew the door through which he'd emerged led to various exits from the house, but he had never before stood on this street, under this mute, alien sky. He assumed it was a part of the property undisclosed to both him and Sister— but why? What purpose would his parents have keeping this part of their domain a secret? Was it dangerous, unused due to some previous incident? Was it a mistake being here?

His mind turned to searching for a weapon. If this place was dangerous he needed to arm himself. After all he'd accomplished, he refused to be killed in this nowhere place. He scanned the street. Saw nothing of value. He would have to search one of the buildings. There had to be something of use inside one of them.

His footsteps were shockingly loud as he proceeded down the sidewalk, drumbeats vibrating against the sky. Shortly, he arrived at what appeared to be an abandoned restaurant. He gripped the door handle, pushed it open with his shoulder. Dust sifted down like a fine snow. A rusted bell let out a dull chime. The interior was dark, washed minimally in the grey light from outside. The place had indeed, at one time, been a restaurant. Tables and chairs covered in white and red-checkered tablecloths, a serving counter. Empty bar shelves on the far wall.

Ryker moved beyond the counter, into the kitchen. The darkness doubled, pressed against his eyes like a physical weight. A stainless-steel countertop winked at him through the gloom. There had to be a knife or similar implement somewhere. Like a blind man, he groped in the dark, hands brushing through the dust that covered every surface. The fryer was filled with thick black fluid that was definitely not grease. It stank of rotting fruit and the musk of dirty, degenerate sex. Ryker choked back his gag reflex.

He moved deeper into the kitchen, toward the storage area. Heard a thump from inside one of the refrigerators. His flesh erupted in goose bumps. His heart tripped and scuttled into his throat. He fell against the wall, arms fanned out as though trying to melt into his environment. Another thump, louder this time, and the fridge door creaked open. A shadow in the shape of a man skulked out in a half crouch. His lips were cracked open and weeping filled the room. The whites of his eyes shone wild and bright in the middle of his murky face. It was then Ryker realized the man was flesh and blood, not a creature of shadow. His naked body was covered in the same black slime that filled the deep fryer. It glistened darkly and dripped on the floor, leaving long black footprints.

Closing the refrigerator door behind him, the man staggered into the open, whimpering like he'd eaten a bag full of razorblades. He stopped a few paces in front of Ryker, who did his best to blend in the shadows, breathing shallowly to avoid being heard. The man didn't seem to notice him...at first. Then his head began to turn with mechanical slowness. Those wild, white eyes alighted on the boy and the man let out a shriek loud enough to shatter eardrums.

Ryker bolted for the exit, his feet skidding on the dusty linoleum. He gripped the doorframe, used it to propel himself behind the counter, which he vaulted, knocking over a stainless-steel napkin holder. It crashed against the floor, popped open and spilled its contents, which fluttered like a swarm of enormous brown moths. The man's feet slapped in pursuit; he slid across the floor with a greasy squeal and crashed into a wall, knocking a series of objects to the ground. Screaming and crying, the man regained his balanced and resumed his pursuit. Ryker reached the door, shoved it open and dashed into the street. A quick glance to left and right and then he was off, searching for a place to hide, a weapon, anything. The restaurant door burst open behind him. The man stumbled into the street, looked around, and upon seeing Ryker, gave chase. He was running full-tilt and would soon catch up, and when he did, what would he do? Kill him most likely. Ryker glanced over his shoulder. The man was closer. His penis slapped obscenely against his thighs as he ran. The sight brought to Ryker's mind another outcome of his capture and he screamed internally at the thought.

With a quickness spurred by panic, his eyes darted in all directions, cataloging the environment, desperately seeking salvation. There were many building and many doors, but the man was so close behind, Ryker couldn't afford to get trapped and cornered. He needed some kind of guarantee that he could slip his pursuant's grasp. Then he noticed the fire escape further down the street. He could work his way up to the roof and maybe...

He altered his course and made for the fire escape. The man was close, shrieking and wailing a few feet behind him.

Ryker hooked a right into the alley holding the fire escape. The ladder was in the up position, the lowest rung more than six feet off the ground. Ryker pumped his legs faster, dove as high as his momentum would take him. The ladder soared into view. He grasped the lowest rung one-handed, twisting his wrist painfully. Gritting his teeth, he pulled himself up, fastened his other hand around the rung. The man snarled into the alley, tripped and reeled excitedly at the sight of prey in such a vulnerable position. Ryker swore, clambered to the next wrung, then the next and the one after that. His feet were almost supported by the lowest wrung, when the man grasped his ankle and pulled. Ryker's chin slammed into the ladder. He bit into his tongue. Blood spurted down his chin adding a new coat of human paint to the rusted metal of the fire escape.

He hooked his arm around the wrung to keep himself from being pulled down. The man screamed and yanked on his foot in quick jerking motions. Ryker kicked out with his free leg. The sole of his shoe met the man's face with a wet thud. The grip on his ankle faltered and Ryker climbed higher. His feet now supported by the rung, he scaled the ladder to the wire-mesh platform above. It clanged and rattled under his weight. He took the stairs, two at a time, climbed to the rooftop.

Peering down, he saw the man jumping for the ladder, arms flailing, but unable to reach it. Relieved, Ryker took a few tired steps before collapsing to his knees. His lungs were on fire, his mouth filled with the metallic taste of fresh blood. He wheezed and drooled crimson into the gravel on the rooftop. After several minutes, fighting nausea and struggling to breathe, he got to his feet and walked to the edge of the building, stared out at the horizon. The building, the street, everything ended a kilometer away from where he was standing, walled off by a buttress of granite sky.

He was trapped. Behind and below him, the man yelled and continued to jump toward the ladder.

7. Bait

Hours passed, but the sky refused to darken. Ryker sat on the roof with his back pressed against the crumbling ledge around the top of the building. His tongue was so swollen it filled his mouth like a fleshy gag. Blood painted his chin and chest and hennaed down his arms. He was trembling with fatigue and the muscles in his legs twitched painfully. All he wanted to do was sleep.

During this time, he determined he had only one means of escape. He would have to double back, find a way to open the door that brought him to this place. That obviously meant falling back into the hands of his family, but it was better than being trapped in this empty world with a man who, even now, continued to shriek and lunge for the fire escape. Ryker knew it wouldn't be easy. The man would follow him back to the door, which brought up another problem entirely. What if he found a way inside the house? The man would no doubt attempt to murder his entire family. Ryker couldn't let that to happen. Even though he desperately wanted to escape their clutches, he couldn't allow a psychopath to rend the lives from the ones he loved most. At the end of it all, despite their differences, they were still Ryker's family.

Before he made his way back to the door, he would have to dispose of the man. The question of how had turned over in his mind for hours, until he realized the answer was right in front of him. He blinked and saw, as though for the first time, the jagged cliff that marked the edge of this world. If he could just find a way to push the man over it, he would secure his own escape and ensure the safety of his family. Once over the edge, the man would simply tumble into the grayness beyond and float there until he stranded on another world—hopefully far away from his family home. That was likely how the man ended up here in the first place, flotsam from somewhere faraway.

All at once, Ryker remembered his dream: the house floating to the edge of the galaxy and beyond, and the alien being staring at him through the bedroom window. Only now, he didn't remember the creature as it was portrayed in his dream, but as the man screaming beneath the fire escape. The substitution filled him with an oily dread.

He got up slowly, and achingly walked to the edge of the building facing the street and bent down to pick up a piece of gravel. It was time to put his plan into action. He lifted his arm into a throwing-ready position and hurled the gravel at a window across the street. It missed and struck the brick frame instead. He picked up another piece, threw it. The window shattered with the ring of breaking glass.

The snarls and screams of the man worked their way around the building, and within seconds, Ryker saw him emerge into the street, racing across the broken asphalt to investigate the noise. The man stared at the shop window, now nothing but a yawning portal rimmed with jagged glass teeth, then glanced over his shoulder. Ryker ducked just in time to avoid being spotted. With a tortured howl, the man stepped over the window frame and melted into the darkness within.

It was Ryker's turn to move. He sprinted to the rear of the building, clambered on to the fire escape, and quietly made his way down the stairs. The old metal groaned under his weight, the railings rattled, but he managed to keep the noise to a minimum. He climbed down the first few rungs and let himself fall the remaining six or seven feet. His shoes scraped the ground and his legs buckled with the impact. Now for the hard part. He would have to lead the man to the end of world while maintaining enough distance between them to avoid capture.

He made his way to the side of the building. Pressed his back against the wall and peered around the corner. The street was empty. The din of screaming and crashing objects came from inside the store. Ryker took in one deep breath, exhaled slowly, and rushed in the direction of the world's end. The stale wind lifted the hair from his brow and blew it about like a funeral veil. Once he was a safe distance from the store, he turned and released a savage cry. It echoed across the cloudscape and flooded the streets and alleys like the roar of flooding waters. In answer, the cacophony within the shop abruptly ceased, and the man came vaulting out the empty window.

Seconds later, he was sprinting in chase. His screams were hoarse from strain. Ryker spared a glance over his shoulder. It appeared the man's feet weren't even touching the ground, so quick and desperate were his movements. Casting his gaze back to the horizon, he saw the edge of the world approaching fast. It came to him that he wasn't sure how he would execute his plan. Did he intend to wrestle or push the man over the edge? Easier said than done. The man was likely imbued with a lunatic's strength and would easily overpower him in a fight. Ryker's anxiety doubled at the realization, but before he could formulate a solution, he felt the man's weight colliding with his back.

He flew forward, smashing hard into the asphalt, his body skidding painfully until his head hung, facedown, over the lip of the world. With the wind knocked out of his lungs, all he could do was gag and gulp for air. The man turned Ryker onto his back, gripped his jaw with one hand and plunged the other down the boy's throat. Ryker's eye widened at the invasion. He felt the man's dirty, jagged nails scraping the lining of his esophagus. The man continued to sink his hand deeper until Ryker's teeth were clamped around his wrist.

Even though tears blurred his eyes, Ryker could still distinguish the man's face. His bone structure was delicate, almost feminine, his teeth decayed. Some even appeared to be sprouting fungal-like growths. One incisor was grey as mildew and bell-shaped, throbbing with unspeakable life. His lank black hair was covered in a caul of filmy pink flesh, like something discharged in afterbirth.

His fingers twitched and danced. Ryker considered sinking his teeth into the man's wrist, coaxing a fountain of arterial blood, but the thought was stillborn before he could carry it over into action. He'd imagined biting the hand completely off, the extremity sliding down his throat, into his stomach where it continued to twitch and writhe like a giant spider. The thought was irrational, but held such power he could do nothing but sprawl helpless as the man probed the secrets within him.

With a violent lurch, the man yanked his hand free. Ryker's jaw clicked. He screamed. The sound was raw, scarred and bleeding. The core of him felt violated, crammed with something dangerous and foreign. He needed to purge, free his body of the invasion. The vomit came first, thick and black and stinking of death. Then his bowels released in a noisy rush, stinking and scalding. Every pore on his body opened like tiny mouths starving for air. From them issued thin, yellow cylinders of pus. As they emerged, they curled and slithered across his arms, down his forehead and into his eyes. He blinked and his tears washed them away.

He stank horribly and in that moment, death seemed more desirable than this state of squalor. His body continued to empty itself, fluids and solids draining out of him like he was a sponge being rung dry. Meanwhile, the man continued to scream, rusty and triumphant.

Through the disgust and exhaustion swirling through his brain, Ryker formulated a plan. It wasn't much of a plan because its intricacies were practically non-existent, but it was sufficient to put an end to both his suffering and the man inflicting it upon him.

He reached up and wrapped his arms around the man. The man flinched, but before he could put up a struggle, Ryker had rolled over the edge. They fell forever.

8. A Feast of You

Halfway through eternity, there was a deafening crash, followed by a flowering of blinding white light. Ryker had the impression of something close to him—the man maybe—blowing apart in a shower of warm fluid. He steeled himself for a similar fate, but before death could claim him, he woke up at the kitchen table, naked and shivering.

His family sat in their respective seats, watching him. He looked up, opened his mouth to utter a question, an exclamation of awe, but his teeth chattered so severely he was unable to speak. Instead, he bowed his head and cupped his hands over his nakedness, abruptly feeling exposed and vulnerable.

Father spoke first. "You should have told us."

Ryker looked up again. Confusion twitched across his face. "What do you mean?"

"The intruder," Father said. "We would have handled it."

He finally understood. His family believed he'd pursued the man on his own. He decided it would be foolish to reveal the truth. He nodded, swallowed the ball of agony in his throat and said, "I saw him from my window. He'd found his way onto the property. If I didn't do anything—"

Mother cut him off. "You could have been killed. If we didn't find your room empty at the exact moment we did, you would have been lost to us forever."

"How long was I gone?" Ryker asked.

"Only a few minutes, I think," Father said.

It had felt like hours. Ryker's mind spun at the thought.

"We thought you ran away again, you dumbass," Sister said.

Ryker shook his head, a show of false disappointment. "I promised you I would never do that again."

Sister crossed her arms. Tears welled in her eyes. She rarely showed emotion—other than the violent outbursts whenever she didn't get her way—so Ryker knew she was being genuine. He was struck by a pang of combined guilt and sadness. And in that moment he knew he would never have another opportunity to escape. He had inadvertently performed an act of penance that would forever bind him to the rest of his family.

Tears of frustration ran down his cheeks. He had failed. Now all that remained to him was the pain. And it was coming again soon.

Mother reached out and caressed Ryker's cheek. "We appreciate what you did," she said, shedding tears of her own. "We were only concerned about your safety."

"I'm okay," Ryker said, his voice sinking below a whisper.

It's over. His fate had been decided. He would have to embrace imprisonment, or be consumed by the magnitude of his failure.

"We love you," Father said. "Sometimes I don't think you see that. But today you proved me wrong."

Ryker's lips twitched into a tentative, improvised smile. Tears cut down his cheeks.

"We *do* love you," Mother said. "Are you ready to give us what we need?"

A pain, cold and hard and cruel, exploded in his chest. He nodded weakly.

Chairs squeaked across the floor. His family stood up. Ryker climbed on the table and sprawled in an X shape, his hands and feet hanging over the edges. Father moved to the countertop, selected the longest of the knives arrayed there—double-edged and newly sharpened—and brought it over to the table. Mother placed a silver bowl rimmed with gilding between Ryker's legs, hunched over and whispered into its basin. Her words echoed and filled the room like the buzz of many insect voices. The ritual complete, she strode to stand beside Father, curling her fingers around his hand that gripped the knife.

"Begin with the meatiest portion," she said, her gaze sliding over her son's naked, sweat-slicked body.

Father lightly extricated himself from Mother's grasp and lowered the knife until its point danced across the flesh of Ryker's pectoral muscles. His scant amount of hair whispered against steel. The blade was cool, like a chip of ice. Ryker barely noticed it. He closed his eyes and waited for the pain. The knife was so sharp—the edge so keen—he felt nothing but warmth as it divided the skin beside his armpit and looped around under his breast. When it pierced the muscle, scraping gently against the slats of his ribcage, the agony flared bright and fierce.

Ryker had grown so used to pain he was practically a connoisseur. Every sawing motion of the knife, every thrust, every rending of flesh and muscle, carried with it its own complex profile. Like a sommelier rolling wine against his pallet, Ryker could differentiate the agony produced by a carving knife with that of filleting blade. The latter was what he liked to call a slow burn: a sting that gradually became an inferno. The carving knife, however, was more brutish, bruising, like fist condensed into a plate of sharpened metal. The slits it opened in his body were also wider, more receptive to the stinging tongue of the outside air.

The pain he now experienced, as his Father lifted the breast meat dripping and steaming from his body, was familiar. His chest was rich in flavor, the muscle lightly seasoned with a marbling of fat; it was a favorite so far as his family was concerned. Ryker had tasted it once, long ago, out of a sense of curiosity. He understood then why his parents needed him, craved him. His flesh glowed with vitality, making him an important part in the continued survival of his kind. He was the provider, the life force and the heir that would ensure the existence of the family.

Father placed the meat in the silver bowl. Blood glittered like precious stones against the polished metal. Mother whispered to the lump of flesh. It shivered in response.

"Father, can I have my turn now?" Sister asked, extending her hand and twiddling the fingers.

He handed her the knife. She placed her free hand on Ryker's forehead, applying enough pressure to hold his head in position. Her palm was sweaty and smelled vaguely of modeling clay.

"I didn't win the heart," she said. "But that doesn't mean I can't take one of your eyes."

She levered the blade into his left socket, angled it slightly so that the orb bulged outward. Ryker's vision plunged sideways as his eyeball jumped free and dangled down the side of his face. Sister picked it up using her thumb and forefinger. It was extremely uncomfortable, but Ryker no longer had access to his eyelids to blink the molesting fingers away. Sister positioned the knife next to the optic nerve and severed it with one rapid stroke. There was a flash of pain like a lifetime of migraine headaches abridged into a fleeting rush of sensation. His vision in that eye went crimson, then white, then out altogether. Sister raised the orb to her lips, the nerve dangling like a string of spaghetti, and popped it into her mouth. Ryker heard it crunch between her teeth, saw the vitreous humor dribble down her chin.

The carving lasted most of the night. When it was over, there was nothing left of him save his skeleton—emptied of marrow—and a few choice organs his family tended to avoid. Included among these was the brain, which rested intact within the bloodied dome of his skull. His family refused to eat it for two reasons: the first being that removing the brain would result in their son's death, while the second held that if they ventured to sample even a mouthful, the grey, spongy flesh would likely kill them.

Though he couldn't hear it, blood dripped steadily from the kitchen table. The floor was flooded with it. Crimson tides flecked with churned foam lapped against the cupboards as his family moved about the space, partaking in the feast. The silver bowl was piled high with his meat. Several water glasses were arrayed along the counter, each containing a unique bodily fluid. A glass of urine glittered like dark lemonade. The lymph beside it, topped with its own foam, looked like diluted iced tea.

Sister reached for the glass of lymph. She was covered from head to toe in blood. Her uneven teeth chinked with shreds of meat. She raised the glass to her lips and drank as though her thirst were endless. Within seconds, the contents of the glass had been drained, and Sister loudly slammed it back on the counter.

Father and Mother were likewise bathed in their son's blood. Mother had taken to lapping it from Father's face. He delighted in the sensation, standing there in the middle of the room with his eyes closed.

Everyone had eaten well. Their bellies were full to bursting. The remainder of the meat and marrow would be stored in the basement freezer for later use. Mother made an excellent stew with the meat from her son's thighs. There was enough to carry them over until the next carving.

As his family finished their meal, Ryker tapped one skinless finger on the tabletop. A single tendon remained that allowed him to accomplish the movement. Soon his body would begin to regenerate. He could already feel the healing properties emanating from his bones. Within days he would be whole again—weak but functional. Sleep would become his closest companion. And just when his energy would return in full, his family would approach him once again, demanding their fill. And this time, he wouldn't run away. He wouldn't challenge his role in the family. There was no way out. He had no other choice but to love them, and to be loved by them—be it with molars and tongue, or with the twisted machinations of their hearts. He would be a good son. He would take care of himself to ensure his flesh was healthy and flavorsome. After all, his family could not exist without a son from which they could feast.

ACKNOWLEDGMENTS

I would like to take this opportunity to thank everyone who contributed to the creation and publication of these stories:

John Skipp, Sean Costello, Stephen King, Jack Bantry, S.C. Burke, Cameron Pierce, Max Booth III, Lori Michelle, Sam Richard, Emma Johnson, Lucas Mangum, Charles Austin Muir, Rebecca Salazar, Emmett Turkingon, Carrie Bertin, Leza Cantoral, Christoph Paul, Melanie McDonald and the rest of my family and friends for your love and support.

ABOUT THE AUTHOR

Brendan Vidito is a writer from Sudbury, Ontario. His work has appeared in several magazines and anthologies including *Dead Bait 4, Splatterpunk's Not Dead, Strange Behaviours: An Anthology of Absolute Luridity* and *Tragedy Queens: Stories Inspired by Lana Del Rey and Sylvia Plath.* You can visit him online at brendanvidito.com

Twitter, IG, FB @brendanvidito

ALSO BY CLASH BOOKS

TRAGEDY QUEENS: STORIES INSPIRED BY LANA DEL REY & SYLVIA PLATH

edited by Leza Cantoral

DARK MOONS RISING IN A STARLESS NIGHT

Mame Bougouma Diene

NOHO GLOAMING & THE CURIOUS CODA OF ANTHONY SANTOS

Daniel Knauf (Creator of HBO's Carnivàle)

IF YOU DIED TOMORROW I WOULD EAT YOUR CORPSE

Wrath James White

GIRL LIKE A BOMB

Autumn Christian

THE ANARCHIST KOSHER COOKBOOK

Maxwell Bauman

HORROR FILM POEMS

Christoph Paul

NIGHTMARES IN ECTASY

Brendan Vidito

THE VERY INEFFECTIVE HAUNTED HOUSE

Jeff Burk

HE HAS MANY NAMES

Drew Chial

CENOTE CITY

Monique Quintana

THIS BOOK AIN'T NUTTIN TO FUCK WITH: A WU-TANG TRIBUTE ANTHOLOGY

edited by Christoph Paul & Grant Wamack

Printed in the USA
CPSIA information can be obtained
at www.ICGtesting.com
JSHW082353140824
68134JS00020B/2054